DARK HILLS

HOLLOW
CLOCKS

stories from the Otherworld

DARK ✦ HILLS
HOLLOW CLOCKS

stories from the Otherworld

GARRY KILWORTH

MAMMOTH

This one is for my grandson,
Conrad,
who put some childhood magic
back into my life.

Part of the author's royalties
have been allocated to
the Cystic Fibrosis Research Trust

First published in Great Britain 1990
by Methuen Children's Books Ltd
Published 1993 by Mammoth
an imprint of Reed Consumer Books Ltd
Michelin House, 81 Fulham Road, London SW3 6RB
and Auckland, Melbourne, Singapore and Toronto

Copyright © by Garry Kilworth 1990

The right of Garry Kilworth to be identified as author of this
work has been asserted by him in accordance with
the Copyright, Designs and Patents Act 1988

'Dogfaerie' was first published in 1989 by Methuen Children's Books
in *Hidden Turnings*, edited by Diana Wynne Jones

ISBN 0 7497 1048 9

A CIP catalogue record for this title
is available from the British Library

Printed in Great Britain
by Cox & Wyman Ltd, Reading, Berkshire

Contents

Dogfaerie   7

Dark Hills, Hollow Clocks   17

The Dragon Slayer   29

The Goblin Jag   42

Warrior Wizards   54

The Sleeping Giants   66

The Hungry Ghosts   74

Changelings   81

The Orkney Trows   90

Scarecrows   103

Dogfaerie

There is some folk what say there ban't no such creatures as faeries, but I knows different, see. Them folk is cockle-headed, as any totter, diddycoy, pikey and tinker would tell. Here's a tale as is proof of such.

More'n a hundred years since, a travelling man took himself from a life on the seaways to settle in the county of Rutland, far north of here. This man built himself a big house on a hill, making use of the woodland trees what covered his estate. While the house were being built, the seed of a dogfaerie blowed in from the woods and growed down below the floorboards. Soon after, afore this wildrose faerie were able to let go its roots, the forest were cut back to a spinney, situate too far from the dwelling for the dogfaerie to reach. There were no escape for the little creature and it were trapped, tight and hard. Leastways, there were *one* way it could get out, but that were a drastic method, which the dogfaerie were not up to using at that time.

In the beginning, it were happy, see. The master married and filled the house with children, fizzy as lemonade, and the dogfaerie's eating habits were such it gobbled their feelings, the way we would a hunk o' cheese and bread. Them were days when the house smelled of fresh-cut timber and the oak and elm were still in it. The dogfaerie were much like a shrunk child itself, with gold tracers in its eyes, a-flashin' like polished brass on a harness.

Come winter the dogfaerie would curl up in the fire ashes, after all had gone to bed, to keep out the cold. Summertime, though, would find it crawling a-tween the kindling sticks, which was not likely to be touched at that point in the seasons. Fireplaces, with their stacked logs and smell of the forest, is true heart-o'-home for dogfaeries, and where they spend much of their forevers.

O' course, when folk was about the house, it spent much of its forever in hiding. It had the magic of shapechangers, so long as there were a copying image in sight, near human form. Like a statue or painting and such. It would stand close to, its eyes burning like candle-flames in a draught, and make itself into a copy of that painting afore burying itself deep in the brushstrokes. From that hidey-hole it would set to studying the folk coming and going, as snug and safe as woodworms in a beam. Folks would look on the eyes of such pictures and shiver a while from their toes without knowing the wherefores.

On such close-to lookings from human folks, the dogfaerie took to having feelings what bant known to you or me. It were both caught and thrown by such close proximities, since it liked the nearness of human folk but hated the stink of a real living soul. One Edward Ruttersdown, owner of this house at the century's change, would lean with his back up at the fireplace, warming his trouser-seat, never knowing what gases wafted from his soul and all but choked the poor dogfaerie's delicate senses.

Later on, of course, the house were full of photos, pictures of the family, old folks and babes, and the dogfaerie would flit from one to other, changing places as quick as a weasel swapping holes.

Listen in, though. There were one image what frit that dogfaerie more than Oberon himself: its very own likeness. When it stood to, afore a mirror and looking on its own form, it knew it were standing on the cliff edge of nowheres – of nowheres in nothingworld. A dogfaerie is eternal, never dying, but take away itself and there is nothing to hold it inside. If the dogfaerie went into its own image, inside the mirror, it would vanish away, for a looking-glass picture is only as lasting as the folk what stands afore it, be they human or faerie.

One night in May-time, when the cherry blossom were covering the windowpanes with pollen dust in the darkness, Edward Ruttersdown spoke a few words to his good wife. 'Darlin',' he says, soft as you like, 'the two of we must go from this here house and find another home. Business in London calls us to it, and we must move to the big city.'

'Oh,' she says in a voice what is tight with feeling, 'and why might that be?'

'The business,' he tells her, 'has got to have me near it, now it's growed so big. There is a grand lady by the name of Wuthers, wishing to buy this old house with good cash. I will buy you a fine home in the town. I know you will like it as well as this one.'

'Well,' she says, looking around wistful like, 'I don't know as I'll like no place as well as this, but if it's got to be I won't cause no argument. But let me tell you this, Teddy Ruttersdown, I shall miss our home, despite its funny ways.'

The dogfaerie were naturally very saddened to hear these words from the human folk of the household. It wanted to make them stay but such power were not in its tiny hands. It could do many things, play many tricks with light and shadow, and send whispering voices from the woodwork of empty rooms. It could drive out spiders, silver the flies and gild the cockroaches. It could copy the bats and birds in the attic, their sounds, and leave peculiar scents in the corners of the hall. But it could not make the humans stay and be happy with their lot.

'And another thing,' says Alice Ruttersdown, as she looks up from her embroidering to the photo of her mother above the fireplace, 'have you told this Wuthers lady that the house is haunted with a ghost? No, I can see it in your face you haven't.'

'Well,' says her Teddy, shifting his bottom as the hot coals send up steam from his shiny pants, 'it would only give her the frits, and she's an old lady. The ghost won't harm her none and she's a very short-sighted woman, deaf as a post with it.'

'Come away from that fire before it scorches,' says Alice. And Teddy does as he's told in such small matters as this, knowing he has got the big one under his wing.

So the house fell into the wrinkled hands of its last mistress. Widow Wuthers were an ancient piece of flesh, dry as a husk of corn let lie in the sun. Her body had not the spark of the child still residing: all her feelings was stale and untasty, leaving a bitter flavour on the dogfaerie's tongue. The dogfaerie came to loathe her bad, since she would chase off young people what come to the garden. Once it even showed itself, but she spit at it and raised up her stout hickory-stick as if to strike. She were concerned by nothing in this life, for death were waiting not far off, crouched and ready to jump on her shoulders, and this squatter in her home worried her no more than ghosts or faeries.

The Wuthers woman did nothing to make repairs on the house and slowly the place fell into ruins from where it would not rise again. When the unwelcome squatter finally leapt and bore her creaky frame to the floor under its weight, the garden had growed tall with weeds what choked the air and fluffed-up the drainpipes with white seedballs, the window-sills of the house had rotted and new tenants moved into the cupboards on insecty legs. Widow Wuthers were taken away to her last narrow home, but no new folk came to fill the old place and stock its larder with tears or laughter.

Silence unpacked its bag and settled in.

The dogfaerie had a melancholy hunger. It missed, most of all, the scampering feet and voices of the children. Now it had only the wind in the chimney. Mice scuttled to and fro behind wainscots and nameless birds stamped across the roof, hollering at their own kind. On occasion, slates did death slides down the roof, to crash on the paths underneath. Moss crept in through chinks in the brickwork and toadstools growed on the inside ledges.

In the shafts of light what sparkled with dust, the dogfaerie sat and moped, its spirit growing lean. All around, the house shed its finery and the damp of the cellars moved up to the bedrooms.

The dogfaerie hated it. And it were not too long afore this hatred sizzled and spat like it were frying in grease, and this meal of emotions it were cooking were intended to be served to human folk, once they came into reach again. Humans had built the house, had trapped the faerie inside one of their dwellings, and lastly, had left it there to pine and starve. On days when Jack Frost twinkled in the grasses outside the windows, and copied the patterns of ferns on the panes themselves, the dogfaerie would go to the great oval mirror standing proud in the hall and think about what shouldn't be thought. It would take to staring at itself, its shape, born of dogrose and bryony during a stalking moon, and try to summon up its strength to enter nothingness, never getting there.

One day in spring it sat licking the cobwebs clean of housefly terror, when it seen two figures come into the garden. One were a tall man with black hair and a face bearing the marks of eighty winters. The other were a small boy with seven summers in his eyes. This pair had come in the grounds through a gap in the old red brick wall where ivy had tore out the mortar. They had fishing rods in their hands and they talked in high voices of finding the large pool half-hidden by thistles.

'This is a good place,' says the boy. 'An't nobody been here for years, have they, Grandpa? You can see that from the thistles. Nobody likes thistles in their garden, do they, Grandpa, eh?' And he laughs.

Fifty years since, the dogfaerie would have loved to hear that laugh, but now it rose fury in it. There were happiness outside, in the wilds of outdoors. It wanted to get to the little boy and poke his eyes out with a twig.

'Can't argue that, little man,' says the child's companion. 'Shouldn't think nobody's been here since the old woman died, when I were a boy. Long climb up that hill. And not much when you get here, except a few old crab apples. Place is filled with wilderness.'

'But it's got this here pond,' says the boy.

'Yep, the pond looks good. Shouldn't wonder there's a fish or two, 'neath that scumweed. Get a line out, boy – let's see what's what.'

So the pair settled in to fish and chatter the sunshine away, while the dogfaerie fumed in the dust and damp of the house.

Later that night, when a rash of stars lighted up the garden, the dogfaerie set to scheming. There were one way it could leave the house, but it meant giving up its faerie form forever. It could, should it wish, take over and possess a child. In the same way it entered images, it could change its form to resemble the little boy and then take over his body. But to do this terrible thing, it had to get the child inside the house.

It gathered from all the nooks and crannies of the house the cast-off feathers of birds. It took some moss from one of the sills in the larder, and some clay what had seeped through cracks in the cellar walls. With these it wove a strange bird, which were sure to catch the eye of the little boy. The tail feathers was all of different lengths and the wings like the flaps of a child's kite. The beak were the tip of a dead rat's tail and the eyes come from two black beetles. Dried spiders made up the claws and its breast were fashioned of dandelion down, blown in fresh from the garden.

The dogfaerie put this decoy just inside the doorway of the house, where the great door hanged loose on its hinges, and waited for the return of the small boy.

The couple did not come for many days and though dogfaeries is eternal, time passes by as slowly for them as any human folk when nothing but expectancies float in the still air around their heads. Its tiny heart were pattering fast as it doodled with a splinter in the dust, waiting, waiting.

Just when hope were all but dry mould in its breast, it heard the sound of voices on the breeze. Into the sunlighted garden come the boy and his grandfather. They stared at the house for a handful of moments and then the boy tugged at the man's sleeve and pointed at the pond.

They sat down by the water, amid cow-parsley, and began to fish. Once or twice the child looked towards the house, but he showed no desire to wander near. The afternoon drifted away and the dogfaerie took to agitation. All it knowed of children told it that the boy would come, that boys like this was curious creatures by nature, following in the footsteps of cats.

Then comes that magical time, just near to sunset,

when windows catch such violence as twilights want to offer, showing red and fierce reflections in the panes. The human folks showed no signs of leaving. Indeed, the man were intent on his line, fixing the fish with his determined stare.

The young boy, however, were watching the clouds of midges coming in, and the low-flying martins dipping in to meet them.

'Hey,' cries the boy, jumping up on his feet. 'Look, Grandpa, the house is on fire!'

The man looks up, briefly, but says no, it's only the sunset snared by the window-glass.

'I'm going to look,' cries the child, and begins running to meet the house, while the man shouts to be careful, not to go inside as the boards is all rotten.

The dogfaerie's heart, small as that of a shrew, twitters inside it. The boy were coming. He were running to the house.

The boy stands at the bottom of the wooden porch steps, which lay at all angles and even have weeds poking sly heads through steps and rise.

Up! Climb up!

One foot on the bottom step, testing for strength.

Yes! Yes! Come. See the pretty bird.

Small light feet, finding their way to the top, to stand on the porch.

A hand on the crumbling doorjamb, skin as soft, pink and delicate as the vanes of a mushroom.

See. See. Look at the pretty bird.

The child's eyes open wide and blue as autumn skies.

'Hey! There's somethin' here. There's a funny bird…'

'Be careful,' calls the man.

'It bant moving. Just sittin' still.'

'Mind the boards,' says the man.

One foot –

two feet –

inside.

The dogfaerie flashed bright as new gold, inside, quick as quick. Inside, deep inside the boy. The boy were caught, the boy were . . . something were wrong. The dogfaerie felt the boy's feelings, thought the boy's thoughts, and knowed that there had been no surprise. The child were in a thrall of triumphant feeling, knowing what he already knowed would happen.

'GOT YOU!' yells this boy, dashing from the house and down the wooden steps towards the man what stands, broad in his smile, by the pond.

'Grandpa, Grandpa, I got him.'

There is slaps of delight.

'I just knowed you would. From the first day we see the house, I said there were one inside, didn't I, boy? It looked so right. No ghost, said I – that's one of *them* in there.'

The boy looks up into the man's face.

'Will I live forever too, Grandpa? Now I've got him? Like you, Grandpa?'

The black-haired man with the gold-flecked eyes ruffles the boy's hair.

'Sure you will, son. And anybody says to you they don't believe in faeries, why you can tell 'em different, see. You can tell 'em the truthfulness of the thing.'

And that's what I done, here in this book.

Dark Hills, Hollow Clocks

My house is silent for a reason. The clock cases of my large collection of antique timepieces are now empty. Outside are the dark hills of Lancashire, equally as silent. I sit here in the dusk of my cottage parlour watching the smooth movements of the greatest clock of them all, as it disappears behind a crag, and wonder at my loss of fortune. I am too bemused to feel anguish at the moment. I am trying to sort through a puzzle, the solution of which will only satisfy my curiosity, not my frustration.

I have been collecting clocks for some twenty years, beginning with my first pay packet on leaving school. I went home with seven pounds, three of which was spent on the silver-cased pocket watch from the window of Jackson's junk shop. My *affairé* with timepieces began in earnest from that day. I find them fascinating instruments, with their precision-made wheels, springs, levers, rachets, cogs – delicate, yet needing strength for durability – but not until I was established in business did I have the funds to indulge seriously in their purchase.

Clockwork movements are the art of the engineer. Not for me paintings by the Impressionists, or sculptures by the Dadaists, or even functional architecture by the Bauhaus school. I love the look of brass behind glass, ornate ormolu cases, tulip-wood grandfathers, faces with curlicued hands, centripetals on the frame, Roman numerals, deadbeat escapements, waggon-spring movements, pendulums, chains and weights, *tick-tock-tick-tock*, sounding brass and tinkling cymbal, dropping the quarter hours like metal lizards shedding their scales. I love moon and tide phase dials, and the dainty spiralling hairspring trembling with the ecstasy of its task. I love the rods and bells, the little hammers, that sound the chimes. I love, most of all, the precision, the teeth of the cogs fitting together like the fingers of tiny hands...yes, tiny hands...tiny hands. They were taken, all, all taken, by tiny little hands.

Last year I purchased a cottage in Thrushgill, attached to an old watermill no longer in use, and brought all my clocks up from the flat in Lancaster. I had metal grids fitted to the windows, and electronically operated bolts on the doors, until the place was as secure as a bank. All my hard-earned wealth was in these precious clocks and it was necessary to keep out any intruders.

I fought hard for my brass, as we Lancaster folk call it, and was determined to become a rich man before I was thirty. Made it too, a couple of years ahead of time. I began as a lowly engineer, but finished owning my own company, and if I had to tread on a few fingers on the way up, well, that was in the nature of the thing. Business is like that, isn't it? If it hadn't been me, it would have been someone else, someone even more determined, more ruthless. You have to recognise what you want and go for it, and if you pause for sentiment, you're lost.

Competitors had to go, too. You see, my factory

turns out good traditional Lancashire cotton: one of the last firms to make a success of such an enterprise. A few handouts were necessary in the beginning, to stop the flow of imported materials, from India and places like that. Eventually I got my way and cleared most of the competition. But there was one, a locally produced muslin, so fine and light it could have been fashioned from dandelion fluff and cobwebs. Some cottage industry I guessed, up in the dark hills behind Thrushgill. It was a superior fabric, I could see that, but it wasn't exactly going to drive me out of business since, judging from the amount on the market, it could only be produced in small quantities. Being a jealous young man in those days, I didn't like losing *any* corner of the business, no matter how small, so I tried dropping my prices for a while, to attempt to force this rival off the market. I was only partially successful, but left it for more important things, such as expansion and increasing my exports.

One or two actions, I must admit, I now regret. There are men who are waiting patiently, simply to be around to stamp on my grave. I don't blame them for that. My ex-partner Joe is probably one of those. And people I've had to let go in my time, though I've never regarded myself as morally responsible for families, only for fulfilling my legal obligations as an employer. You can't afford to be emotional in business, or you go under. Never married. Never had time.

Then I bought the cottage in Thrushgill, near a rushy beck that tumbles from the crags. It has a long garden – something I've not owned before, always living above the offices of my factory – and I took some books out from the library in order to learn something about growing vegetables. I've never had much time for flowers, but producing one's own fare for the table, well, that's another thing.

The problem was, the garden faces north, so the shadow of the cottage is on it in the morning, and in the afternoon it is in the shade of those dark hills. However, I did my best with it, buying all the latest fertilizers and weedkillers and such. I don't hold with many modern innovations (*especially* quartz movements and digital watches: cold, soulless bits of wire covered in plastic), but it's my belief that one should take advantage of improvements in agriculture. This I duly did.

Right at the far left-hand corner of the garden is a wedge of ground where the midday sun manages to strike, as it slips between the corner of the house and the first crag of the ridge. It was here that I planted the blackcurrant bushes, in well-drained beds of peat and manure, dug and prepared as the book tells. They would have flourished, if it weren't for the blackfly.

'You need some poison dust,' old Wacker, the local authority on such things told me. 'A puff 'ere, a puff there. Give 'em a good going over. That'll knock the blighters for six.'

This I duly did and was successful in ridding the bushes of blackfly.

Then I had problems with birds, stealing the early fruit. Having no protective nets to hand, I decided to dust some of the blackcurrants with poison dust, to teach the birds a lesson. It was a cruel thing to do, I see that now, but at the time I was very angry.

The following day was a fine summer's morning. Going down to the bottom of the garden to inspect the bushes, I found to my horror a small corpse lying on the ground under the blackcurrants. It was the body of a pixie, no doubt come down from the dark hills to steal the first of my fruit. My heart went cold. My grandmother had always told me that Lancashire fairies were normally benign creatures, who would never harm a child, but terrible if roused to fury.

'They have the patience of eel grass,' she said. 'You don't want to go upsetting the fairies around here, lad.'

I had taken the life of a pixie! Unwittingly, perhaps, but would the fairies listen to my explanations? I very much doubted whether I would even be invited to my trial.

The pixie's body was smaller than that of a weasel: perhaps twenty centimetres long. I picked it up, quickly, and took it indoors, placing it on the scullery shelf amongst the flower pots and seed trays and other garden paraphernalia. There were some onions drying in there, and woody geranium stems that I had not cleared away. I placed these over the corpse, hiding it from view. Lancashire fairies are wild folk and have great difficulty entering human dwellings. My cottage is more secure than most, so I felt safer having him indoors. If I had just buried him, they might have discovered his grave.

That evening, I sat at my window, fearfully

watching for small hands, small faces, to press themselves against the glass. I could imagine the grim expressions, the angry brows, and my knees trembled at the thought that they would come in their hundreds to drag me out to the crags to carry out whatever ghastly punishment such creatures devise for killers of their kin.

They did not come.

For several days I stayed in the cottage, neglecting my business in Lancashire, afraid to go beyond the doorjamb in case they were waiting for me amongst the ferns and grasses. Then, gradually, I came to the conclusion that no one had seen. Soon I was able to go out into the sunshine, and walk again through thickets and down amongst the gulleys. However, when I went to work I always double-locked the windows and doors, and blocked the chimney flue, to prevent any unauthorised entry of my property. They would need more than fairy guile to get past *my* guard.

Autumn came, then winter, and that February I took Wacker on as my gardener. I didn't want any more accidents to fall on my head. Wacker knew what he was doing amongst the weeds and vegetables. He had the knowledge of more than one lifetime, passed on by his earthy ancestors. Wacker liked to come in and look at my collection of clocks from time to time, and would shake his head in wonder, exclaiming, 'Aye, like flowers of tin and tinsel, Mr Roberts.'

He would stand and listen to them chime, as if he were at a concert, listening to the world's greatest orchestra playing Mozart or Handel.

'Sheer delight,' he would whisper. 'They could be fuchsia bells made o' copper and brass.'

Once, in mid-winter, I inspected the little body hidden on the scullery shelf, to find it had dried, just like a small cutting. The legs had become a fork, small knots where the knees had been, the two arms little twiggy projections from the main stem, and the long hair had shrivelled and looked for all the world like root tendrils. It seemed to have taken on the characteristics of both the geranium stems and the dried onions.

I put it back in its hiding place and forgot about it.

In the spring, I was full of myself. Business was booming. The cloth from the cottage industry, that flimsy but strong fabric which caused me small worry, had dropped away on the market to almost a rarity. Wherever it was located, the weavers were running out of something – probably raw materials.

My garden was flourishing under the green fingers of Wacker, who produced prize vegetables out of the most unlikely soils and positions. I had time to relax and oil my precious clocks. There was the Thomas Tompion in the study, the George Prior late eighteenth-century tortoiseshell with its small marine view above the face, my Breguet's *synchroniser* in the landing window niche, the French cartel, the English brass lantern-clock by Fromanteel made in 1670, and many many more. I loved them all. My heart lifted when I had time to work on them, tinker with them, keep them running smoothly.

One evening I came home to find a beautiful plant on the upright pianoforte. It was in an ordinary clay pot which had been placed on a cracked china saucer to protect the polished wood surface of the instrument. The plant had a faintly familiar appearance, though I had no idea what it was. There was just a single bloom, a magnificent scarlet trumpet-shaped flower, so heavy its stamens almost touched the surface of the piano.

Wacker was working at the bottom of the garden and I called him up to the house. He came up the path kicking the soil from his boots and then entered the scullery.

'Where on earth did *that* come from?' I asked him, pointing to the plant.

Wacker shifted his feet on the stone floor of the scullery as he peered around the parlour door at the plant.

'She's a beauty, that one. Found 'er on the scullery shelf, four little branches, just sproutin' green. Put 'er in that pot, and there she be.'

Suddenly, the cosy feeling of well-being left me and a chill travelled through my whole body.

'But the flower, Wacker. It can't have bloomed in one afternoon, surely? When did it grow its flower?'

Wacker shifted his feet.

'Didn't *grow* it, like normal, if you see what I mean. After I potted 'er, she kind of *bled* the bloom. That's *best* way I can describe it. Sort of oozed out a drop o' red sap on stem. When I come back in, an hour later, there she hung in all her glory.'

Horror replaced my feelings of perplexity.

'Throw it out,' I said, coldly. 'Now, you idiot. You should never have potted that...that *thing*.'

'What?'

'Throw it away, Wacker,' I shouted. 'Didn't you hear me?'

Wacker turned, and left me, saying, 'I heard all right, I ain't deaf, but I ain't being spoke to like that.'

He slammed the door behind him.

I stared at the vile flower, that had grown from the husk of the dead pixie, and wondered if I would have the courage to throw it out myself. It was getting late. The purple lanes of the last shadows were stretching themselves on the lawn. Light drained from the sky, swirling down some invisible sluice behind the dark hills to the northeast.

'In the morning,' I murmured, tossing my jacket over the back of a chair. 'In the morning I'll take it out and burn it on a bonfire. Should have done it ages ago.'

I spent the evening tinkering with a banjo clock and retired at eleven o'clock, thinking I would have to apologise to Wacker for my outburst. I planned to tell him I had been unwell and was not entirely responsible for my show of temper. Wacker was not one to hold a grudge and I was sure he would forgive me.

Some time later I woke with a start, having heard my name being called. I felt groggy, as one does when awakened from deep slumber. Putting on my dressing-gown, I went down the wooden staircase to see if there was anyone at the door. It occurred to me that Wacker might have been downing some ales at the local pub and had called by to put things to rights. As I reached the bottom step, all my clocks began chiming. Although I am used to the sound of their ticking, and their chimes, and am not awakened by them, for some reason the tinging and donging put fear into my heart. Twelve times the clamour repeated itself.

Midnight.

I stood on the final stair, looking into the eerily-lit parlour, wondering. Why was I so frightened? What was it in here that made me so anxious?

Then I heard it.

'*Mr Roberts. Mr Roberts. Murderer.*'

Terror almost clogged my throat, but I managed to cry out, 'Who's there? Who's that?'

The words came again, from the direction of the piano, and I knew then what it was. The trumpet flower had called me from my bed. Its high tones were informing the world that I had carried out a deed as yet unconfessed. A full moon sat in a saddle between the dark hills beyond Thrushgill, illuminating my parlour, picking out my furniture. I saw the scarlet blossom tremble in the light.

'*Mr Roberts!*' it shrieked.

Then they came.

At first, specks of light amongst the thistles, then small white faces at the windows, breathing chlorophyll, handprints like raindrops on the panes. They began rattling the glass, shaking the door on its hinges.

'*Mr Roberts!*' cried the scarlet trumpet. '*Murderer!*'

The violence at the windows and doors increased.

I put my hands over my ears, yelling, 'It wasn't my fault. I dusted for pests. It was an accident...an *accident!*'

But they would not go away, they would not leave me alone, and in the end I had to let them in. I flung open the door, shouting, 'Don't hurt me. Don't touch me. Take what you want, but leave me here, please, leave me alone...'

They were silent then. They poured past me into the recesses of the house and began to dismantle my precious clocks. Four or five fairies at each device, quietly removing screws and pins, and taking out the works of each of my antique timepieces. The shells, the cases, they left behind, looking as if they had not been touched. Even the dust on them was undisturbed.

The fairies took the scarlet trumpet along with the vital innards of my priceless collection, and headed back for the dark hills. Leaving me, broken and bereft, amongst the silence of my hollow clocks.

That was over a month ago.

Sitting here now, staring at those hills, I have an idea that I may have been hoodwinked by those little people. You see, that fine muslin has begun to appear on the market in much greater quantities than ever before. Consider this, if you were to make a loom for tiny hands, it would have to be scaled down in size, would it not? All its parts would need to be in miniature: its cogs, levers, rachets. Fairies, we know, are not metalworkers, nor even good carpenters. Their skills are inclined towards more delicate creativity, like weaving. Any machinery they need, they have to modify from an existing contraption, perhaps originally fashioned for some entirely different purpose.

In short, I am now certain that my clockworks have become looms, or parts of such. In this day of the quartz movement in clocks and watches, those creatures out there must have despaired of finding replacement parts for the looms they have run over the previous several centuries. Now they have enough to last them for many years: my whole beautiful collection of antique timepieces.

What bothers me is whether it was all a fairy plan. Surely not? It was so elaborate, so full of chance. Too much was dependant on human reaction and odd circumstance.

Then again, are we humans not predictable creatures? Any animal that knows us, be it cat, dog or bird, can easily foretell what action we will take in any particular circumstance, even the most unusual of situations.

And are not fairy schemes, by the very nature of their planners, full of such embroideries as would startle any mortal with their twists and turns, their loops and twirls?

I don't know. I just don't know. I simply have the feeling, as I sit amongst my hollow clocks, staring at those dark hills, that I have been duped in more ways than one, since I have lost my precious collection of clocks and my business is fighting against the upsurge of an old rival I thought I had knocked out of existence.

It's a blessed puzzle, like some cobweb left on purpose over the staircase, that sticks to your nose, your eyelashes and your brows, and gums your fingers, as you try to sort through it.

The Dragon Slayer

Only a handful of years ago, in the British Crown Colony of Hong Kong, people still believed in dragons. Indeed, the name of the district called 'Kowloon' means 'Nine Dragons' and was taken from the range of hills which separates this part of the peninsula from the New Territories in the north. Of course, European *gwailos* scoffed at such beliefs, since they had known for many centuries that dragons were mythical creatures which had existed only in the minds of men. Foremost amongst those who looked with contempt upon such archaic convictions were the officers of the Hong Kong police force. One of the younger officers was in charge of the top section of Kowloon, just under a hill known as Lion Rock.

The young man's name was John Witherstone and he was a keen, ambitious policeman. He was blond, tanned and had a fine set of white teeth that set off his smile very well. His superiors thought he would go far and this made him slightly arrogant towards his subordinates and colleagues. Though he was not universally liked, and knew this, he was not terribly concerned. He expected to make a few enemies on his climb up the career ladder and as long as he was popular in the right quarter he was not too worried. Once he had more power, it would not matter if he was highly regarded amongst the other *gwailos* or not.

Gwailo is the term given to people of European origin by the Chinese. It means 'devil people'. When the British first heard of this nickname they had been given, far from being insulted, they were amused and began using it to describe themselves. There was even a football team called *The Gwailos* from Hong Kong Island. John Witherstone did not like being called a *gwailo*, but then he had very little sense of humour. His colleagues called him 'stoneface', though not in his hearing, because he had a fierce temper.

One day, up in the hills of the New Territories, a tribe of farmers known as the Hakka People came across a dragon sleeping in one of their orchards. They immediately got together and asked each other what was to be done.

'If we wake the dragon, he might burn down our orchard,' said one farmer.

'And possibly eat a few people afterwards,' said another.

'On the other hand,' said a third, 'we can't leave him where he is because we have to harvest the fruit very soon.'

They decided to try to wake the dragon, but in order to placate it they placed gifts all around its sleeping form. There were baskets of oranges wrapped in gold paper and pears wrapped in silver. There were red and gold paper banners, these being the lucky colours, planted in the earth. Colourful kites adorned the trees and wind chimes made from seashells hung from the branches, tinkling musically in the breezes. Red lanterns with gold fringes had lighted candles glowing from their hearts, the smell of incense perfumed the air. Beautiful pyramids of painted eggs were placed at the four corners of the orchard.

When all was ready the villagers created a great cacophony of sound, clashing huge brass cymbals together and beating giant kettle drums with wooden spoons. Primitive instruments like one-stringed violins wailed around the hillside, gongs sounded and bull-roarers bellowed. Ancient bronze trumpets, not used for a thousand years, blared their dirty-sounding notes. Bamboo wind-instruments moaned and groaned, and hollow gourds sent mooning notes into the rocks and around the terraces.

The Hakka People played their instruments on tip-toe, ready at a moment's notice to run like the wind once the dragon woke. The dragon hardly stirred. The players stopped after three hours, exhausted, with chapped lips, numb fingers and ears that rang with bells like those in high mountain temples.

One very old lady, whose face was a map of wrinkles hidden by the black fringe that Hakka People wear around the brims of their hats, had this solution to offer.

'We need a demon to drive out this dragon from our orchard. What we need is a *gwailo* with great authority, who will come here and tell the dragon to leave.'

This advice was accepted with much nodding of heads and murmuring of tongues. A group of three farmers was despatched to Kowloon to request the assistance of the most important *gwailo* in the area, the police officer John Witherstone. Reluctant to miss the chance of having a procession, the rest of the village marched behind their spokesmen, waving bold flags and singing brave songs.

August in Hong Kong is the worst month for humidity and heat. John Witherstone was sitting in his office in his starched khaki uniform sweltering under a slowly moving ceiling fan. He was dreaming of icebergs and snowy wastes and thinking of the long cool drink awaiting him at his club after duty finished. While he was immersed in such thoughts, one of his Cantonese policemen, Peter Li, knocked on his open door.

'Step inside,' said Witherstone curtly.

'Sir,' said Constable Li, 'there is a group of Hakka farmers to see you, from the New Territories. They seem very upset.'

'Can't the desk sergeant deal with it?' said Witherstone, not bothering to keep the impatience out of his voice.

'Sir, they make a special request to see you. They say they must talk to an important man.'

John Witherstone felt mildly flattered.

'Oh, very well, show them in, and stay to interpret for me, constable.'

'Yes, sir.'

Hats in hands, the trio of farmers was ushered into the small office and stood smiling nervously before the great man. One of them had been elected to speak and he explained their problem and requested the assistance of the mighty officer in driving away the dragon from the orchard. John Witherstone listened in silence as his constable translated this message into English. Finally, he rapped his stick on the desk top.

'Isn't this just a little ridiculous, constable?' he asked of Peter Li.

'Sir?'

'This dragon business. I mean, surely these people don't still believe in mythical beasts in this day and age. Good God, this is the twentieth century, not the Middle Ages.'

Peter Li smiled and said, 'These are simple people, sir. Their beliefs are still strong in these matters. Of course, your constables do not believe in such things – we are civilized men of the world – but these farmers . . . some of them have never been more than ten miles from their village. The world passes them by without leaving them a good education.'

'Hmmmmm.' John Witherstone regarded his desk top and then the shy faces of the farmers. 'And sending a sergeant and a couple of men to investigate this *dragon* will not satisfy them?'

'No, no, sir. Certainly not,' said Peter Li hastily. 'It must be someone of great importance.'

John Witherstone weighed up the advantages and the disadvantages of proceeding with the request. On the one hand it would be hot and dusty up in the New Territories, but there was countryside there, hills and valleys and stretches of water. Such scenery would make a change from the streets of Kowloon. Then he had to decide whether his superiors would consider him a fool for following up such a request. It would not do to lower his stature in the eyes of those responsible for promoting him.

He picked up his phone.

'Wait outside,' he waved his hand at the Chinese. 'I'll give you my decision in a moment.'

Peter Li led them out.

A call to his immediate boss gave John Witherstone all the justification he needed to make the trip up into the New Territories.

'Find out what it's all about, John, will you? I mean, what seems like damn tomfoolery to us is taken seriously by the Hakka. We don't want to upset them and it's good for our image, to be seen to be taking a firm interest in the local culture. You'll probably find a dead monkey up there or something. Make the most of the situation. We need to be seen to be doing "good works" on occasion.'

'Yes, sir.'

Witherstone put down the receiver and shouted to Peter Li, who stood in the doorway once again.

'I'm going up to investigate,' he told the constable. 'You and another man come with me.'

'Me, sir?' said Peter, turning a little pale.

'Yes, you sir. Come on man, get your skates on, we haven't got all day. Order me a Land Rover from the car pool.'

So up into the New Territories they went: two unhappy policemen, three relieved farmers and one grim *gwailo*.

When they arrived, the police were led up to the bottom terraces of the orchard. The villagers said

34

that they were convinced that the dragon was Jek Lai, one of the smaller but ferocious brothers of the great Jek Mai. John Witherstone said he would see, once he and his constables got to the top of the terraces, where the dragon was sleeping.

With the two Cantonese policemen clutching their rifles, John Witherstone led the way up through the orchard. There, at the top, he came across a remarkable sight. There was a reptile of some kind, stretched between two fruit trees. It had a long body covered in scales, but its head was a monstrous size. There were two horns protruding from its brow and its skin was covered in colourful patterns which John Witherstone recognised after a few moments. Its eyes were wide and staring. The creature had obviously just woken up and it began to move.

One of the policemen gave out a startled cry and immediately retreated back down the hill, despite an order to remain. The other, Peter Li, stood his ground, but his legs were shaking and once he had looked on the form of the dragon, he refused to do so again, averting his eyes.

Contemptuously, John Witherstone took the rifle from the hands of his constable, levelled it at the beast, and shot it between the eyes. It writhed on the ground for several minutes before finally succumbing to the inevitability of death. Peter Li was then ordered to collect brushwood and build a pyre, on which John Witherstone burned the body of the dragon. When the villagers came up, the charred remains of Jek Lai were there for them to see and they were both shocked and horrified.

Peter Li translated their fears to John Witherstone.

'While they are pleased that you have destroyed the dragon, they fear for you, sir. You were not expected to *kill* the creature – merely drive it away. Now you will be hunted down by other dragons. They are calling you the "dragon slayer" and are admiring of your great prowess as a powerful mortal. Your name will be made famous, and stand amongst the names of heroes who have slain dragons in the past . . .'

John Witherstone waved his hand.

'It was nothing,' he said.

Privately, once he got back to his desk, he telephoned his boss once again.

'It was only a snake, a big python that had half-swallowed a young cow,' he told his superior. 'The cow's horns were sticking through the skin, giving it a kind of ugly, distorted appearance. I must admit I was a bit startled until I'd had a better look. One of my policemen did a bunk straight away. Can't say I blame the beggar, though I'll have to put him on report.'

'Your fame has preceded you,' said his boss. 'They're already calling you the "dragon slayer" on the island. One of my boys has just been in to tell me how the great white hunter slew the beast.' His boss laughed. 'You're a local folk hero. This won't do you any harm, John. I shouldn't be surprised if you don't make a little on the side out of this.'

True enough, the next morning the gifts began to arrive from all corners of Hong Kong. Officially, officers in the colony's police force are not permitted to receive gifts, which might be regarded as bribes, but Witherstone declined to send them back. After all, some of them were very valuable items – gold watches and jade jewellery – and there was no harm in becoming rich on the way up the ladder to success.

It was almost six months later when another group of Chinese came down from the New Territories to ask for the assistance of the Dragon Slayer once again. One of the villagers had been eaten and the dragon had disappeared into a large cave in the side of a mountain. The people were fearful that the dragon would reappear and wanted John Witherstone to match his legendary skills against the beast. Since his earlier success, John Witherstone had been bragging about his prowess with the gun.

'I slew the dragon Jek Lai,' he continually told new recruits, and they pursed their lips because they knew the four winds will always carry a boast to the ears of one's foes.

With his tongue in his cheek, the *gwailo* set forth again, this time without his two policemen. He was shown the cave entrance and then the local people retreated to what they regarded as a safe distance, at the foot of the mountain. There was the sound of distant thunder in the air and the *gwailo* looked up in search of dark cloud, but the sky was clear. He was glad, because he did not want to be trapped inside the cave if it rained hard and swelled any underground streams which crossed his path.

John Witherstone had taken the precaution of

bringing with him a torch. He also had his revolver, which he considered adequate for the task. No doubt there was *some* kind of creature in the cave which would require shooting, and he could think of nothing dangerous enough in the area that could not be disposed of with a hand gun. The tigers had long since gone. It was probably another snake, or some mangy cur that was half mad. The thing to be wary of was a hound with rabies, but he was a good shot with a pistol so he need only be careful of being taken by surprise.

He entered the cave expecting it to be quite shallow, like most of those in the district. However, it became obvious that it went beyond the normal length as his torchlight probed the darkness and found no rear. After a while he came to a fork and decided to begin laying a trail, so that he did not get lost. Like the Ancient Greek hero Theseus, who had to find his way out of the labyrinth which held the Minotaur, John Witherstone used a ball of thread. He tied one end to a rock and unravelled it as he went through the left-hand tunnel. There was a faint smell of sulphur in the atmosphere of the cave, but this did not worry him at all.

Instead of narrowing, the tunnel began to get wider and John Witherstone could hear running water in the distance. He had already had to negotiate one or two pits in his path, had climbed a rock chimney and was on his way through a passageway full of stalagmites and stalactites. He was beginning to consider turning around, since it seemed doubtful now that he was going to catch up with the animal that had gone into the cave, wherever it was. All he need tell the farmers when he got out, was that he had slain the dragon and they had no more need to worry. Of course, if the creature went out again and hurt someone else, his credibility would suffer enormously and his reputation would not be worth a hoot. So he had wanted to be sure that the animal was not going to reappear.

Just as he was considering following his line of thread back to the entrance, he felt a warm breeze on his cheek. There had to be an exit ahead, for the air to be getting into the tunnel. He had already seen one or two living creatures, snakes and bats, which indicated that the outside world was not too far away.

Sure enough, as he turned the next corner, he found himself in a huge cavern with a high ceiling. It was dimly lit by cracks of sunlight. When he had climbed the rock chimney he must have been going upwards, alongside the wall of the mountain. There were fissures in the rock face, which let the daylight in. Water trickled through the limestone on the far side of the cavern.

Suddenly, there was a movement somewhere in the cavern, and the chamber echoed eerily with the sound of stones dropping from a ledge. John Witherstone flicked his torch backwards and forwards over the floor, rapidly, in an effort to find what had caused the noise. The torchlight revealed many distorted and frightening shapes, but these were the result of water erosion and the build-up of calcium deposits on the limestone. There were cathedral-like flutings rising from the bedrock and sinister columns with hollow faces. From the distant ceiling hung giant stalactites that looked at any moment as if they would fall and bury their points in the ground beneath.

'Nothing here,' murmured John Witherstone, to reassure himself. 'Must have been the water or something.'

Then, as his sight became used to the natural light, he saw a huge form on a ledge on the far side of the cavern. He strained his vision to define its shape. It seemed narrow at both ends (one end more than the other) and wide of girth in the middle. Once he had some points of reference, he calculated its length at around a hundred metres. Two large red-rimmed eyes regarded him balefully from above a set of hissing nostrils. In the dimness he could see what looked like the wings of a giant bat, situated about two-thirds of the way along the body, towards the head. The wings fluttered as he stared, giving out a leathery rustle. On the end of the one muscled, scaly leg he could see, was a terrible three-toed foot with claws like the blades of ancient scythes. A row of triangular spikes ran from the creature's terrible head to the tip of its tail, which ended in a thorn-shaped point not unlike that of a scorpion's sting, except that it was the size of a man's arm.

'What. . .?' cried John Witherstone, but the rest of his sentence was swallowed up by a thunderous roar. The great jaws opened to reveal a thousand daggers, and the beast spoke.

Its language was as old as the dust in the heart of the cave and not understood by the *gwailo* police officer, but there were those further down the mountain who heard it, and knew what it meant. They understood that terrible retribution had at last caught up with the slayer of dragons, and if they had been asked for a translation of the sounds that came through the fissures in the rock and rolled down the mountain scree, they would have said, without hesitation that these were the words they heard:

'The wind tells me that you slew my brother Jek Lai.'

The Goblin Jag

Some people believe that goblins can party anywhere, but that just isn't true. I should know. I've made a very close study of these fantastical creatures and know more about them than most. Clym-of-the-Clough, who lived with goblins for many years, was a good friend of my several-greats grandfather. Fairies, elves, hobgoblins, pixies, cluricaunnes, dybbuks, kobolds – these creatures all need special circumstances to come together. A place where elemental forces meet and mix. I'm not familiar with *all* the necessary ingredients for a goblin jag, but I do know three things that *are* essential: a forest, a place without people and an aeolian harp.

These three elements, and one or two others, were present when I got caught up in a goblin jag. It's a lonely place, a place without people, that's certain. I'm talking about the rooftops in an area of town where tenement buildings, some six to eight storeys high, are built very close to one another. So close you can jump over the alleys from one block on to its neighbour, providing you have longish legs.

The forest is a forest of television aerials: thousands of them all clustered together: thin metal saplings that sway in the breeze.

Finally the wires that support the poles create an aeolian harp: when the wind blows through them they hum strange melodies. Archaic pibrochs, ancient gigs, fit only for the ears of supernatural beings.

Of course at first there were only the old-fashioned H-shaped television aerials, but since then some marvellous things like the skeletons of giant leaves have taken the place of these earlier models. The rooftop goblins love this filigree forest of rods, poles and aluminium foliage. They see themselves in a metal jungle, a place where alloy palms and steel ferns grow so densely you can lose yourself amongst them. This is where most of their jags take place, there being few woodland forests left these days. Especially on goblinfest nights when just about every kind of fairy wants to break dance until the dawn. Unfortunately for the tenement dwellers these riotous assemblies are most active during prime television time and cause glitches and razzles to zaz across the screens and interfere with favourite programmes.

It was these zig-zag or wavy lines that told me one night in the late nineteen seventies, when I was about fourteen years of age, that something was up on the roof and messing around with our TV aerial.

My name is – well, you don't want to know that – you won't recognise it anyway. It's a good Scottish name and one of which I'm proud, but we've no Rob Roys to boast of and the clan tartan is as common as purple heather. I live in an old tenement in an area known as Murdoch Mansions, set on a rise at the back of Edinburgh. Like most people in those days, I watched a lot of television and since my parents went to bed early, round about nine o'clock, I got to view the spy thrillers and such. Anyway, one night I was really into an old Hitchcock film about ten o'clock, when the screen started acting up. I began getting a load of fuzz at first, then wavy lines, and finally the picture went on the wonk.

Now, our rooms are on the top storey of the building, so I went out of the flat into the main hallway and found the back stairs. These led to a doorway on to the flat roofs of the tenements. Not suspecting anything awful, I opened the door and stepped boldly out into the night.

It was a full moon and I could see the beams glinting on the forest of aerials as I tried to make out which one was ours. I thought perhaps a bird was using it as a perch for the night and was having a touch of insomnia, tossing and turning, trying to get to sleep.

Of course, once I was up there I could tell it was an impossible task. There was no way I was going to find our aerial amongst that lot. A quarter of Edinburgh's television receptors were stretched out before me. They were so thickly planted a sparrow couldn't have flown a metre inside them without stunning itself. Had they been real saplings they would have grown sickly and thin through lack of space and light. It was a wiry tangle of metal antennae. Nevertheless I waded in, finding a path under the prongs, hoping to scare away any birds that might be amongst them. Suddenly, I came to a small clearing near the edge of the roof where a fearsome sight lay before my eyes. I was stunned into stillness.

There must have been about two hundred

goblins, all frozen in the act of violent motion. They had obviously been in the middle of a frenetic dance – goblins can work themselves up into a real frenzy when they're enjoying themselves – and on hearing the rooftop door open they had stopped dead. Every one of them was staring at me with a ferocious expression. I had never seen such a wild bunch before in all my fourteen years. They looked more hostile than a tribe of Mohican Indians out on the rampage.

Now, normally fairies have perfect camouflage, but goblins are the exception. Rather than blend with the world, they dress to clash with it. They are aggressive and rebellious creatures who roam in packs looking for light mischief and like the other fairy folk to see them coming. One thing my highland grandfather always impressed upon me was the saying, 'Never fall foul of goblins, laddie, for they are not of a forgiving nature.'

And here I was, interrupting one of their jags.

I turned to run, but got caught up, the prongs hooking my jumper like branches, the projecting screws catching on my trousers like thorns. I was held fast by the metal forest, which seemed to be acting in accord with the goblins' wishes, as if they were using it to snare me and stop me escaping their fury. Soon they were all over me, dragging me back to the clearing, and I don't mind telling anyone who asks that I was terrified. I thought they were going to eat me at first.

One of them, with purple spiky hair, seemed to be the leader and he walked up and down in front of me, his tiny stubby thumbs stuck in his hip pockets, and glared into my face with such malevolence it had me quivering like one of the television aerials in a high wind. Goblins, of course, regard their nightly doings as very private, certainly not for human eyes. Dire punishment is meted out to those who dare spy on them.

It was hopeless calling for my parents, though the urge to do so was very strong. They were extremely deep sleepers. And there was no point in trying to apologise: how do you get to speak to goblins? They have a harsh demonic-sounding tongue which is within the pitch of the human ear but which I believe would be impossible even for a language expert to decipher, even with modern computers and such. It would be like trying to say sorry to a pack of baboons.

Terror was squeezing my heart now, with strong bony fingers. I wanted to run, but there was no breaking that circle. I couldn't even lift my foot. They had robbed me of all power of movement. Then I began to hear goblin voices in my head. They obviously wanted me to know my fate. The accents were hard and rasping. They might have been members of a Glaswegian street gang chatting over the fate of a victim.

'See this whan? Whut'll we do wi' him?' said one.

'A nice new haircut for a starter,' replied another.

I felt my scalp tingle all over.

'A few wee baubles, ah think.'

My nostrils quivered and my ear pinged.

'Whut aboot a gude jacket?'

I felt a breeze around my chest and my shirt, tie and blazer I knew were gone. Something clammy and slick was next to my skin. A further, heavier garment went on top of this.

'N' the breeks. Gie the scunner some braw new breeks!'

My grey school flannels followed my other clothes into oblivion and some rough material replaced them. I tried to look down but my neck felt as if it were made of stone. I couldn't move my head.

'Extra ventilation whid do nay harm.'

I heard the cloth tear in several places, mostly around the knees and at the bottoms.

'Ornaments for the trews?'

Something clicked into place around my thighs.

'He cannae walk aboot barefoot. Gie him some clumpers, see.'

My feet were suddenly in agony and I tried to yell.

'Och, the boots are tae sma' fer the laddie.'

The tone was sarcastic but a moment later the pain went away as I felt the footwear expanding.

'An' that's that! We've got oorsel's a new Puck, laddies.'

The last sentence had a final ring to it. I was suddenly very relieved. Whatever they had done to me could be undone within minutes once they let me go. I would take off the rags they had dressed me in, climb into bed, get a good night's sleep, and dress properly for school in the morning. Nothing to it.

Except that they weren't going to let me go.

They called up the wind and the wires began to play their strange shrill music. The jag started again, and it was instantly compelling. My feet began a jiggidy kind of dance, moving faster and faster, until

I was jumping and spinning, hopping and leaping, along with the best of them. Two hundred small lumpy creatures in ragged colourful clothes were bouncing like crazy all around me, their limbs moving swifter than the wings of sparrows in flight, their coats flailing, their heads bobbing. I danced and danced, my heart bubbling with excitement. 'Yeeeehhaaaaa!' yelled a goblin next to me, flashing me a terrible goblin grin. 'Yeeeeeehhaaaa!' I responded, full of the ecstasy of motion. I could do this dance! I could jounce and jigger along with the best of them. They screamed with delight as they went even faster and I managed to keep up with them. They shrieked with joy when they bobbed and weaved, and spun on their bottoms, and I followed their example. It was a night of jubilation, of celebration.

When the dawn crept over the edge of the rooftops my eyes began to feel heavy, my limbs weary, my head full of mercury. Never mind undressing. Never mind the bed. I would lie right down where I stood, on the roof, fully clothed, and sleep off the exhaustion that had washed through me, filling my veins with quicksilver.

When I opened my eyes I was in the assembly hall at school. Surrounded by my schoolfriends I was aware that hundreds of pairs of eyes were on me alone. Up on the stage were the teachers, and their expressions would not have been out of place on church gargoyles. The headmaster was standing at the microphone. His eyes bulged, his face was red, his body quivered. He gave the impression that he contained tremendous pressure, that his temper was about to cause an explosion.

Unfortunately he finally found his voice.

'BOY!' he shrieked, the sound coming out like steam from a ship's whistle. 'GET OUT! GET OUT!'

Was this a dream?

'GO!'

My ears rang with the shrillness of the shout. This was no dream. The goblins had transported me to the morning assembly. This was tomorrow. I was in the middle of my school chums and they were staring at me as if I had three heads.

I turned and began hobbling towards the back of the hall, to the swing doors. I say 'hobbling' because my thighs were chained more tightly together than they had been at the jag and it was difficult to walk properly. I tried to retain some dignity but I knew from the round eyes that followed my progress that I was no ordinary lad. Not any longer. Had the goblins given me a donkey's head? Frog's features? Rat's whiskers? Something was very wrong with my appearance, which surely could not have been due just to the clothes I wore.

I clinked and squeaked straight to the boys' locker room and stood in front of a full-length mirror. Breaking out into a sweat I could see why the headmaster had been a little upset by my appearance. I could see why my friends looked at me as if I'd grown flippers where my arms had been.

My head looked as though it belonged to a cockatoo. It was shaved high on both sides, leaving a ridge of hair standing up like a brush on a Roman centurion's helmet. It was dyed orange and green. There was a safety pin through one ear and another through one of my nostrils. I was sporting mascara and not just a dab or two. My eyes were ringed with black. My shirt, if it could be called that, was simply a black plastic waste bag with armholes cut into the corners. Over this was a cracked leather jacket covered in symbols, some of which would be sure to make my gentle father go berserk. Below the waist I had on thick faded jeans that were full of elongated holes. There were three toilet chains attached to them at the thighs. On my feet was an enormous pair of boots.

I looked, in fact, like a giant goblin.

They had simply transformed my appearance so that I looked like one of them. Added to this, they had written a word on my forehead in purple ink. I think it was meant to say 'Puck', the nickname they had given me for the night, but goblins are notoriously bad at spelling. What it actually said was:

PUNK

No wonder there had been such a fuss out there. No wonder everyone had been staring at me with such horror.

Or had it been horror? When I thought about it, I could have sworn there had been something else in those eyes, something quite foreign as far as I was concerned. I had seen such a look before, in the eyes of first year boys who stared at the school soccer team captain. I had seen it in the eyes of teachers congratulating a pupil on getting into Oxbridge. I had seen it in the eyes of girls who were seeing a friend off to the national athletics.

It was *admiration*.

Have you ever wondered where fashion comes from? I don't mean French or Italian fashions, designer label stuff, but *underground* fashions, the street-wise trends. The sort of thing I'm talking about is when you see a teenager wearing something really enig, something absolutely weird, like a plastic face mask and a yellow boot on one foot and a pink shoe on the other, and if you're between twelve and twenty yourself you think, zam-bam plastic man, I'm going to get some of that, I wanna be a rebel too. Have you ever wondered who dreams up this kind of stuff? How it *seems* just right for the time, is tasteless enough to annoy adults yet feels good when you drift around in it? I mean, it must bother you that everyone else starts wearing this sort of gear before you even get to hear about it. How does the word get around so quickly? How come you wake up one Saturday morning to find that all your best friends are dressed in crazy clothes you've never seen before while you're still in yesterday's wear? It was never on television or videos or in films, that's for sure. The media don't get to show it until it's way out of date and something new is on the streets. Even pop stars follow, not lead, in underground fashion. Where does it come from? I'll tell you where it comes from.

It comes from *me* and I wish it didn't.

*

I was sent home of course, and my parents gave me hell for a few days. They made me wash the dye out of my hair, but they couldn't do much about the Mohican haircut itself. That had to stay. At school I was threatened with expulsion, but then the headmaster relented. What I got was extra work, which probably didn't do me any harm, though I resented it at the time. After all, it hadn't been my fault.

Still, the goblins weren't happy. You probably know why. Next Saturday morning there were at least a dozen kids out on the streets wearing what became known as 'punk' gear. That dozen grew to several hundred in the Edinburgh area and eventually reached London and the rest of the world. These days, though punks are way out of fashion, you will even find them in remote places like Raratonga or Hong Kong. You see what the goblins forgot, what all fairies *constantly* forget, is that whenever they interfere with a human and change his or her appearance, they leave something behind them. It's difficult to give this fairy residue a name, but it's something like glamour or charm. Some might call it fairy dust. Whatever it is, the effect on other humans is always the same. They are fascinated by the result. They might be repulsed by it. They might find it attractive. They *definitely* find it fascinating.

So, to many in Edinburgh, I was a hero. I was a fashion leader or what they call a charismatic. People began to ask my advice on all sorts of things, not only trends in dress, but other things as well, stuff I knew next to nothing about. They began quoting me. I had to be careful what I said in case it got distorted.

I was an underground fashion star. A cult figure.

The goblins were dead annoyed at this.

Some time after I became a punk I moved down south, to start a new life, but they got into my bedroom and transformed me yet again, as indeed they did many times afterwards, when much to their fury I went from success to success.

This second time they made me look like a certain type of English goblin. One of those that live on the rooftops of Manchester or Liverpool. They shaved off *all* my hair leaving nothing but a head of skin. They tattooed a tiny bird on each of my cheeks and put an earring in one ear. They gave me a thick plaid shirt and trousers that were eight centimetres too short in the leg. The trousers were held up by old-fashioned braces. My big boots remained.

I'm getting a bit old for this lark now.

Warrior Wizards

You surely recall what a strange time we had of it, that summer when the plant life went mad? Being a gardener o' course, I put it all down to some new artificial fertilizer at first. Some counterfeit product gone out of control. I've never understood what was wrong with all the good old bone-meals, silage and manures. They're forever bringing out new expensive brands of unnatural fertilizer, and researchin' even more in them laboratories up near London, and I thought, 'This time, me old cockers, you've gone and done it for sure.' But it weren't that at all. It were something quite unusual for these parts of the Chiltern Hills.

It turned out to be a war between two wizards.

Now, I'm no story teller, not as such, but since I'm the only one who knows what's what in this tale, I expect I've got to be the one to tell it. It's no good me passing it on to one of those writer people, because their minds get too fanciful, and every time they recount the thing, they add their curlicues and traceries, flourishes and fiddleheads, 'till the *real* story gets buried under lots of fake new growth. I'm here to tell the tale with weeds an' all, no dung needed, neither.

What happened were this.

My little cottage is a ways out of a village up in the Chilterns and I wakes from a tidy sleep one early

morning to find the house coming apart at the
seams. Jaggedy cracks of daylight appear in the
walls and the sun jumps through, eager to chase the
dark from the corners. Spiders blink and scurry for
hidy-holes and a great feeling of alarm sweeps
through the beetles scrambling in the wainscot. I
have to admit to myself that under my own vest is a
parcel of unease. I think it's the bulldozers and
cranes come to knock down my little cottage like the
council threatened. 'They've come,' I say to myself,
and wonder why I can't hear the thump of the big
iron ball on the end of its chain, as it cracks my home
open like a goose egg.

On closer inspection, however, I see what the
matter is. All the wood in the cottage: the beams
supporting the roof and walls, the joists, the doors,
the window frames, the jambs, everything wooden,
has sprouted green and is beginning to grow. Dead
wood is springing to life and throwing down roots
again. Knotty planks is warping and twisting,
pushing out branches, and posts reach down into
the rich clay below the floorboards, to find water.

Outside my kitchen window the herbs is going
mad, with angelica and marjoram, tarragon, dill and
coriander, rosemary and feverfew, all struggling
with each other as they fight for light. A rhubarb
stalk thrusts rudely through the open doorway,
bearing a leaf as large as any tropic palm. All around
the house the turnips and carrots and potatoes are
battling for survival as their neighbours encroach
upon their soils.

Pulling on trousers and shirt for decency's sake,
though there isn't a neighbour 'till beyond the ridge

of beeches near Greensall Gap, I rush outside, scared of being brained by falling bricks. Once out in the air, I'm able to get a better look.

The place is a jungle.

The lane that leads on past my cottage is being punched from underneath by all sorts of saplings, tufts of grass and thick waxy weeds, some of them I don't recognise. They're growin' fast. One squat little dwarf is becoming a thick-boled, gnarled giant in pretty quick order. I know that one all right. Fig. A fig tree, growing right outside my own garden (which is now up to the eaves of the crumbling cottage), right where I'd spat some pips when hoeing out the cabbage lines. There's others too: twisted old olives, grotesque as ogres: wild tomatoes; melons; pomegranates with tiny leaves and scarlet blooms, apples, oranges. Lots more. And local flora too. Oaks, crack willows, wych elms. By the end of the morning, as I hack away with my sickle trying to stop the advance, I'm watching the fig leaves unfurl and flatten, and seed pods like green fists swell to bursting.

In my own little garden, peasticks sprout, bamboo canes grow faster than the bean plants and garden fence posts is resurrected from the dead. They reach out at life in every direction. My gazebo frame has shucked its glass panels and is like a giant cage of fibrous green. All around me is a tidal wave of tangled wood and stems, flooding the countryside. There looks to be no way of stopping it, and when the noonday sun burns through an overhead net of vines and branches, I give her up and leave her to run. There's enough imagination in me (given I'm not like those writers, with their embroideries), to guess what's happening all over the Chilterns. Bridges collapsing, blocking the rivers; fences so high they blot out the sun; sewage farms, where many seeds end up, blossoming into crammed orchards of every kind of fruit.

I thinks to myself, them professors and their damned fertilizers have done it this time. We should have been satisfied with staying plain organic and refrained from meddling with artificial growers.

Just when I was cursing fit to bring God's heavy boot down squish, on my prize marrows, a man steps out of the forest, and into the little clearing I'd made for myself around the remains of the cottage. He takes out this scarlet kerchief, and wipes his brow. Then, breathing deep, he turns to me and says, 'Phew, a bit of fresh air!'

'Help yourself,' says I. 'I'm not chargin' today.'

He laughs at this and then his face goes all serious again. He's a thin, nervy creature with a small pointy head, but not really unusual for the Chilterns, since we get all shapes and sizes round these parts. We're a kind of crossroads for the south, and every vagabond, traveller, pedlar and hiker leaves a footprint outside my door *sometime* in their wanderings. I look at my hand, covered in grime, thick-skinned and cracked. If I make a fist out of it, his head is smaller than this. His own hands look pale and silky, like candle wax, and I take him for a clerk or bank teller, lost on his way from town to town.

Then the little man stares at a telegraph pole near to where he's standing.

The painted and creosoted woods have sprung to life just same as every other, but chemical preservers soaked-up by these timbers produce blossoms in the way of hybrids. The oils have got deep into the very spirit of the tree, and out have come dark-souled flowers in morbid hues. Blooms to be fingered by a dying emperor, or to drape the dead of an inglorious battle.

A thin rare shaft of sunlight has found its way through the treetops and spotlights a huge rich-purple blossom with yellow stamens. The strange spiky petals are covered in bees that murmur secret messages to each other in the noonday heat.

'There's nothing quite so beautiful,' says the little man, still staring, 'as a telegraph pole in full bloom.'

Then he turns to me and shrugs.

'I'm lost,' he says.

'I'm not surprised,' says I. 'Lived here all my life and don't recognise a bit of it. The world's gone mad. It's them damned professors and their fertilizers.'

"Fraid not,' he comes back. 'It's Waggelifel. We were meant to have a battle, tonight at midnight, and he's trying to stop me getting to the combat site.'

'Waggelifel?'

'My enemy. I'm a wizard, you see,' he says, sitting on a stump that proceeds to carry him gradually upwards while I watch. 'The Chilterns belong to me – in the sense that there should only be one wizard to each range of hills – but Waggelifel is making a bid for my territory.

He's been pushed out of the Cotswolds, and so . . . now it's war.'

He wipes his face again with his red kerchief, then starts to knot the corners.

'Who're you?' he asks, when I have nothing to offer.

'President of Holmer Green Village Produce Association,' I say, puffing out my chest.

He nods at the leafy screen above and around us, now becoming so dense it's turning the light to a deep shade of green.

'Well, you've got enough produce here, haven't you?'

'Not of my growin',' I say.

'No.' His face becomes grim again. 'Waggelifel's.' He puts his kerchief on his head, like them at the seaside.

'Look,' says I, 'you being a wizard like you say, why don't you get rid of all this with one twirl of a willow switch, like I heard tell of such things? Then you can meet this Waggefly, and knock the aphids out of him with magic or whatever?'

He sighs, jumping down from the stump.

'I wish it were as easy as all that. Unfortunately one needs time to build up sufficient reserves of magic. It's like energy – well, it *is* energy really – and it gets used up. Think of me as a battery that needs recharging from time to time. If I use up all my magic in getting rid of the greenery, I'll have nothing left with which to fight Waggelifel. It would take at least a week to replace it. You see, the *positive* use of magic isn't as draining as the *negative* use. He put the jungles here, but I should have to use much more magic to get rid of them. Sowing the seeds is not half so much work as gathering in the harvest. Do you understand?'

'Not much,' says I, 'but I think I see where your problem sits. You have to find this Wagawillie, but not using magic. Is that it?'

'Perfectly,' he says, with another sigh, 'and I'm beginning to think it's an impossible task. I need to get down to the outskirts of High Wycombe, on to the Dashwood Estates, the cave where the old Hellfire Club used to meet. It doesn't look as though I'm going to make it and I'll lose the combat by default.'

'That depends,' I says, 'on what you're prepared to pay for a guide.'

He looks at me through squinty eyes and wipes himself with his scarlet kerchief. I sense the blackbirds and thrushes, moving closer to hear. The weasels in the blackthorn thickets, standing on their hind legs, leaning outwards, straining their ears. The rabbits, deep in their burrows, holding their breath.

'*You* can find the way?'

'That depends,' I repeat.

'But it'll be dark soon.' He looks around. 'It's already dark in here. How are you going to do it?'

'I'm still listenin',' say I.

'I'll restore everything back to normal,' he says, 'providing I win of course.'

'That's as to be expected.'

'Naturally, and for you my fine friend, President of Holmer Green Village Produce Association, a giant prize marrow that will . . .'

'None o' that,' say I. 'I grow marrows the size of houses without any help from magic. What I want is this. They tell me they're going to pull down my cottage.' I turn and look sadly at the ruins of my dwelling. 'Well, Waggatrump's done it for them. But when you win you'll put it all back to rights, won't you? After which, I want you to stop the council from doing it all over again, and in their case, permanent.'

His narrow face frowns.

'You mean there's a compulsory purchase order on your cottage?'

'*That's* the beggar,' I tells him, poking him with my finger. 'They tell me they want to put a motorway through my garden and they're allowed to buy my cottage and piece o' land whether I want to sell or not. I know that's true, because I've asked. They can buy the home your grandfather gave you, and for a few bitty pound notes. This is *my* cottage, and I'll be damned and buried and damned again before I'll let 'em have it.'

His funny pink eyes cloud over a little.

'Tall order,' he says. 'You know how much magic it takes to tamper with the Town Planning Department? They've got rules within rules, those people. If they don't get you one way, they try another . . .'

'Is it a deal?' says I, folding my arms, 'or do we let Wagtail fly away with the Chilterns?'

He sighs and beams.

'Deal,' he says. 'Let's get started.'

I get some gardening tools, a parcel of cheese, biscuits and water, and off we go, starting at the telegraph pole and working our way through the thick undergrowth to find the electricity pylons that march across the land like giants, from Oxford to High Wycombe, and on to London. Some places we have to cut our path through the undergrowth, with honed sickles, and in one spot we have to use the axe.

I go into a bit of a tiz-woz when we find the first pylon, wonderin' which way to turn, but I can see the dim light through the vines, more dramatic in the west, and turn eastwards to where I know High Wycombe is sittin' waiting for whoever tries to find her. I follow my nose, knowing there's no better compass than the perfume it inhales on its travels. There's more than one way to journey the earth, and the least important sense is sight, when it comes to long geographic strolls.

It's late in the evening when we come to the edge of the town. Everywhere is in a crumpled state and I can but hope my wizard will knock the stuffing out of his opponent, so we can get everything back to rights.

'That way,' says I, 'straight up the hill. When you get to the top, that's the old Lord Dashwood's place. The cave's a bit down from there.'

He shakes my hand, his left eye beginning to turn blood red with determination, ready for his coming combat.

'How did you do it?' he asks. 'Now we're here. How did you find the way through that jungle? I know you followed the pylons, but how? How did you get from one to another when we couldn't see one metre in front of our faces, or above our heads?'

'No real secret,' I says. 'The wires and overhead cables of that there national grid is covered in creepers now, mostly honeysuckle and convolvulus. Heavy scent. You must have smelled it. I just followed the fragrance. Knew it would lead us here, to the edge of Old Wycombe.'

'So simple,' he says, shaking his head and smiling. Then, grim again, 'Well, wish me luck.'

Then up the hill he tromps, swinging his little arms and waving his little red flag.

Round about midnight the sky opens up with thunderous sounds and a cracking, flashing lightning that seems likely to split the heavens open wide enough to let the stars fall out. The earth shakes and heaves, as if it's giving birth, and the rain comes down in great globules full of red dust. There's a screaming going on fit to swallow the cries of a banshee.

While we was walking, I'd asked the wizard had he had any other fights in his time? Oh yes, he says, lots of 'em. It's a bit like a duel. You get three wishes, he says, but it's usually the first that counts. The last fella I fought, I got in first, and wished him deep in subterranean depths. He wished himself above the bedrock, but found himself at the bottom of the sea. Then he wished himself above the sea . . . and found himself in bedrock. It was an *underground* sea. His last wish brought him back to the battlefield, but by then he had used up all his magic and was completely vulnerable. You have to fight a lot, if you want to hang on to what you've got . . .

I thought over all this, while I waited for the combat to end, up on the Dashwood estate.

At seven minutes past midnight, down comes my wizard, pink eyes gleaming and a big grin on his face. He waves his scarlet kerchief at me.

'Done it!' he says, triumphantly.

'What?' says I. 'You won?'

'Turned him into a mortal,' says he, 'and sent him to a hell on earth. When he wakes up tomorrow, he'll find himself a grey little man, in a grey little job, in a grey little office. That'll teach him to take me on.'

'What about all this?' I ask. 'When will it be put back to rights?'

'In the morning,' he calls, as he walks away. 'It'll all be right in the morning.'

And so it was. And having kept that promise, I didn't doubt he would keep faith with the second, more personal oath that he'd made to me.

So it happens at the end of that week, while I am laying horse manure on the vegetables, a grey little man in a grey little suit comes to see me from the Town Planning Department.

'Mr So-and-so?' he says, polite as you like. 'I've come to apologise for an error made by my predecessor. Apparently he placed a compulsory purchase order on your cottage? This has since been found to be wrongly issued and has now been rescinded. Not my fault, you understand. I've only been in the job for a few days.'

His voice is melancholic. He is a small man, not unlike another man I once met, with a nervy twitch and a pointy little head. His face wears a thoroughly miserable expression, as if his job is a hell on earth. He makes a tick on his clipboard, then turns to go.

'Does that mean my cottage is safe?' I ask him.

'Absolutely,' he says.

When he's a bit down the lane, I call to him.

'Better luck next time, eh?'

He turns and takes out a little blue kerchief, wipes the sweat from his brow, and then continues along the track. All around him the dry weeds are crackling in the ditches, the wildflowers swoon in the shade, and the trees reach out in a leisurely fashion, as if gathering in the sunlight with the tips of their fingers.

The Sleeping Giants

Back in the time when what was what, and before things changed, there was a miller who fathered five sons and one daughter. Now, the five sons had several choices concerning what to do with their lives, from joining the army as trumpet majors, to running away to sea, to becoming the mayor of a town. Miller's daughters, however, had but two. They could stay and help their parents run the mill, or they could marry and help someone else's son run his farm. *This* miller's daughter, whose name was Jill, wasn't having either of those. She informed everyone she was going out in the world to build her *own* mill. Her brothers laughed, her parents wailed, but Jill thumbed her nose and set off one dawn when the flour was like powdered stars, still in peaceful heaps on the loft floor.

On the way along the road, she met a wolf.

'So, what's all the hush and rurry?' he spoonered.

Jill ignored him, and since his curiosity was aroused, the wolf fell in behind her and they continued along the winding road together.

Soon they came to a wooden bridge across a stream. As Jill and the wolf were crossing, a troll leaped from the grassy bank to bar their way.

The startled wolf jumped and then put his paw on his chest.

'Don't *do* that!' he said.

66

'Where are you two going?' snarled the troll.

Jill brushed him aside in contempt. The troll looked at the wolf, who shrugged, and the Scandinavian immigrant fell in with them, intrigued by this strange girl with a faraway look in her eyes.

The trio entered a deep, dark wood, where a wodwo had its home in a hollow log. It jumped out on them as they passed along a narrow path and the wolf shrieked and almost fainted.

'What am I?' cried the wodwo, this being the only question he had ever wanted answered since finding himself in a squirrel's drey some seventeen summers ago. He had seen his reflection in a pool: a lump of clay with bits of twigs and feathers sticking out of his head; grasses growing from his ears (if they *were* ears); pebbles and pieces of bark and bracken and other stuff elsewhere on his form.

Everyone completely ignored him.

The wodwo tagged on behind until they came to a dragon stretched across the path.

'Why don't you join us?' suggested the wolf, but the dragon declined, saying that she didn't like the look of the lump of green mud with twigs for hair, which left the wodwo muttering, 'A green? I didn't know I was a green. What's a *green* anyway?'

Finally, the whole group reached a long fertile valley where a giant lay on its side, fast asleep. They walked the whole length of this enormous creature, until they reached its head in the late evening. The wind from its slow regular breathing lifted Jill's hair and made it stream out behind her, yellow and long.

'This is it,' she said, putting down her pack.

'This is what?' chorused the others.

'This is where we build the windmill. You, wolfie, go and borrow some tools. You with the twigs, go and look for a large round flat stone in the river. Make sure it's smooth and when you find one, bore a hole through the middle. Troll, you can help me stitch some sails out of these sheets I've brought.'

Soon the place was an ants' hill of activity. The wolf felled timber with an axe borrowed from a woodsman and the troll sawed them up into long yellow planks. Jill began nailing the planks together. The wodwo took it on himself to do intricate work, like the frames for the sails, at the same time asking curious onlookers if they knew what he was.

Before long the sleeping giant's deep and steady breath, which smelled of freshly-cut herbs and ground peppers, was turning the great sails to Jill's windmill. Farmers began to move to the valley and the fields started to yield wheat, maize, barley and oats.

The giant slept on.

By the following year the windmill was grinding corn and producing fine flour which sold throughout the land. Jill adopted the wodwo, but the wolf (poor devil) was bitten by a strange man at full moon and had to be shot with a silver bullet. The troll became a full partner in the mill.

A passing pilgrim helped the wodwo begin compiling a list of all the things he was *not*, hoping one day to reach an object that could not be accounted for.

Soon the valley began to fill with people.

First came the real estate agents, and the lawyers.

Then a swarm of tinkers and pedlars.

Then the tradesmen and shopkeepers.

A schoolhouse was built, and a church.

Then came a doctor, who was also an insurance salesman, followed by a banker, some oddly assorted police and a man who set up a private sanatorium for broken-down actors.

The postal services moved in.

An old tramp made his home in the giant's hair.

A clocktower was raised as high as the giant's shoulder.

A town hall was erected and a mayor elected.

Homeless aristocrats began to drift in.

So, around Jill's windmill, the sails of which were turned by the giant's dependable breath, a whole town sprang up. In time there were even refuse collecting services.

The giant slept on, surrounded by beautiful buildings and dreaming spires.

An artist sketched the town and a poet came there to die. The townspeople built bridges over the giant's limbs, great sweeping arches that melted into roads. One side of the giant, where the mill stood, became known as Windy Streets. The other, behind the giant's back, was called Calm Hills.

Soon the town became a city and trains were invented. Cars came along and street lights and garage walls and graffiti. The city began to get an overcrowding problem, especially out on the limits where the immigrants tended to settle and where the refuge camps were situated.

Jill retired with the wodwo and troll to a place by the sea, where they opened up a tea shop and a penny amusement arcade. They sold the mill to an enthusiastic intellectual who turned it into a museum. It was painted white, had pretty window boxes, and many visitors came to see its wooden cogs and levers ('In *actual* working order') turned and moved by the sails.

The giant slept on.

In fact, the giant's breath had become a bit of a nuisance. It blew away hats and umbrellas, raised dust and litter, and its constancy was really rather irritating. People preferred to live on the far side of the giant, in Calm Hills, where it was rather more peaceful. The prices of houses in Calm Hills rose steeply, until only the very wealthy could afford to live there.

On Windy Streets, where the giant's snoring breath threw up rubbish and paper, the poorer folks' houses began to deteriorate rapidly. The landlords of these dwellings all lived on the far side of the giant and sent only rent collectors, never maintenance men. After all, *they* did not have to live in decrepit buildings or smell overflowing sewers. Some of them had never seen a rat or a cockroach in their lives.

As properties in Windy Streets fell into disrepair, the larger shops and stores closed down and businesses began to move away. Unemployment rose and there was despair and heartache.

The paint peeled off the windmill and since gangs of knaves roamed the streets looking for trouble, visitors were reluctant to make the journey to the mill any more. A changeling named Stilty Rump bought the windmill for a song, painted it red, and turned it into a night-club. There was a casino at the back, and a restaurant on the second storey. The power was provided by an electric generator driven by the refurbished sails.

The giant slept on.

There were murders and suicides and theft and bribes, all somehow connected with Stilty's mill, though nothing could be proven. Politicians became involved, police were corrupted, and rival gangs raided the windmill from time to time causing bloodshed. This did not prevent the residents of Calm Hills from coming to Windy Streets in their windproof sedans, to gamble and generally have a good time. Then one blowy evening, when the nightingales were singing in the squares, Stilty Rump was arrested and taken to jail. His reign was over.

Stilty's sons and daughters had been college educated and opened up legitimate businesses. They turned the mill into a working model again for the interest and education of school children and overseas visitors. The mill was staffed by long-haired pixies and elves who made wholemeal bread (full of goodness and fibre) which sold to health food shops.

'Windmill Bread' became famous and the mill attracted many people from foreign lands. City officials were constantly harassed by important visitors, asking why Windy Streets was a ghetto. They pointed out that vitelline taxi drivers still refused to take fares to that part of the city.

So, new honest policemen were drafted in to weed out the rotten ones, and arrests were made amongst the gangland fairy folk. Bad politicians packed their bags and left town.

The giant woke up and went away, taking the ruins of several bridges with him.

The windmill closed and became an historic monument.

Two proposals were put forward regarding the space vacated by the giant. One, that it should be used to rehouse people from the ghetto. Two, that it should become a private golf course for patrons from Calm Hills.

The golf course won.

The windmill became a secret bomb factory for a group of anarchist elves called the Gretalites. The buildings in Windy Streets were finally condemned and the tenants and paupers moved out, most of them heading for the coast to run slot machine arcades in the booming seaside towns. Early one morning in May, when the blossom was pink on the bough, there was a tremendous explosion which blew the windmill to pieces. The whole district was flattened. Landowners sold their acres to the *nouveau riche* from the resorts on the coast, who built inland hotels as quiet retreats away from the hurly-burly of the flourishing ports.

A second giant came along.

Seeing a nice soft patch of green turf in the centre of the city, he lay down to sleep, with his face towards Calm Hills.

His foul exhalations whistled noisily down the driveways of the large mansions owned by wealthy landlords and politicians, stirring the gravel, rattling garage doors and blowing topspray from the garden swimming pools. Tennis court nets were whisked away like chiffon scarves and deck chairs and pool umbrellas decorated the trees. Greenhouses and conservatories were flattened. The panels of expensive fences flew like bats into the evening skies.

The new giant had rotten teeth and bad breath.

Property prices fell overnight to rock bottom, and the rich became poor, and the poor became rich. Some might say that was a happy ending if the story stopped here, which of course it never does.

It simply starts again, perhaps with the hotel owner who had five daughters and a son?

Once upon a time . . .

The Hungry Ghosts

Hong Kong at the end of August is at its hottest time of the year and the humidity is such that normally good stiff paper turns limp and damp, and forgotten clothes form beds for fungi at the bottom of drawers. Residents of Kowloon Tong and the more airless districts make excuses to visit Hong Kong Island, so that they take the Star Ferry across a cool stretch of water. British *gwailos* complain wearily to each other about the human condition in those same self-satisfied tones they used back home on cold, wet and windy days.

Perhaps it is because August is a sultry, steamy month which tries both the body and spirit, that Yen Lo, the keeper of the underworld, allows the ghosts out of his domain for twenty-four hours, to visit their relatives. Perhaps Yen Lo believes that his ghosts will find it so unpleasant along the crowded Nathan Road, or in the thick of the masses at Temple Market, that they will be anxious to return to the more acceptable climate of the underworld at the end of the day. Maybe Yen Lo has no need to spend his time chasing runaways the following day, since his charges are no doubt happy to be back home where at least their difficulties remain arid.

Yen Lo's day is celebrated amongst the local population as the Festival of the Hungry Ghosts, and to placate the roving spirits fires are lit in open spaces, and food is left on offer.

At such festive times roadside Cantonese operas blossom in the evening hours, for the entertainment of both the living and the dead.

Richard Tang and his wife Sara drove home from one of these performances in Tsimshatsui, to their new tenth-floor flat on Diamond Hill. They were Christians but they still, like the *gwailo* Christians did with their own pagan festivals, observed many customs and traditions of their ancestors. During the drive they spoke little to each other, immersed in their own particular thoughts. The journey was slow and tedious, as always on the roads of a city which housed six million people. As they travelled along they studiously avoided looking at the roadside fires, which was difficult since there were so many of them.

When they arrived back at their apartment, Richard drove the Mercedes into his personal space under the building and they took the elevator to their floor. Once inside their rooms Sara made some tea and they sat on the balcony watching the aircraft float over the rooftops in and out of Kai Tak, still saying nothing, each still locked into their own private reminiscences. Occasionally one of them would try to glance at the other without being observed doing so. There were problems between them and a barrier had formed like a wall of glass. They could see each other, like a stranger on the far side, but there was no spiritual contact. Each acknowledged that it was not the other's fault, that any blame was mutual, but still there remained this spectral obstacle between them.

Finally, Richard said to Sara, 'Shall we leave some food for the ghosts? What do you think?'

'We usually do,' she replied. 'Why behave any differently this year?' She turned to him, the rattan chair squeaking with her movements. 'I don't think we have very much in the larder. Shall I make something? Some cakes?'

Richard suddenly became animated.

'Why not? And I'll do some sweetmeats. How about that?'

She exclaimed, 'You, cook?'

'Of course!' He puffed out his chest. 'A man can do anything, if he puts his soul into it.'

So they went into the kitchen and set about their individual tasks with an energy that had the air conditioning units working overtime. As they prepared the dishes, incredibly, they chatted to one another.

Unknown to the two adults, their children Tim and Susie had been eavesdropping on the conversation. While the parents were busy in the kitchen, and flour was like vapour in the air, the youngsters hid behind the hall cupboard and discussed these events in whispers with some excitement. Their mother and father were doing something, *together*, at long last. It was a cause for celebration in itself. For six months the adults had hardly spoken to each other. Since moving to their new apartment they had communicated in grunts when they had to, but preferred to maintain silence most of the time. It was as if words were subject to the heavy humid conditions of the weather and the effort of producing them too wearisome. Perhaps at last conversation was becoming less of a strain, less of a torture, and some semblance of normality was returning to the household.

Soon there was an aromatic atmosphere to the apartment. Sara always said that cooking odours were *fragrances*, rather than smells, and tonight the two children understood what their mother meant. Had they not already eaten their fill at their grandmother's not two hours earlier, where they had swallowed sweet-and-sour pork, egg fried rice, Singapore noodles, chilli prawns, glutinous rice, and other dishes, with abandon, the fragrance issuing from the kitchen would have them smacking their lips in anticipation. They were almost sorry, once the cakes and sweetmeats were cooling on wire trays, that they had been so greedy at Grandma's apartment. Had they known what was in store, they agreed that they could have sneaked into the kitchen during the night and sampled the gifts left for the ghosts. Those who have left home will know that there are few things in the world to equal a mother's cakes, and the results of a father's cooking are always interesting, if nothing else.

Sara arranged the cakes on a china plate of floral design, while Richard chose a stoneware dish, plain on the inside but having an exterior pattern, a fishing boat battling against fast-flowing seas. Chinese believe artistic arrangements to be just as important as the taste of the food, and much thought goes into the overall *shape* of the presentation.

Once this was done, the adults retired for the night.

Out amongst the misty crags of Lion Rock, amongst the boulders of Poh Ping Chau, over the natural stone arch known as Hopeless Buttress, the phantoms of the dead roamed at will. They had but a few more hours of freedom, before Yen Lo gathered them in and herded them back to their places in the underworld. They looked down on the tall buildings below, where the religious observances having been completed, paper representations of the gods of hell had been set on fire. Other spectres wandered through the streets, or walked the waterfronts of Aberdeen Harbour, where the junks and houseboats jostled each other for dirty wavespace. In the most densely populated area of all, the Walled City, a giant slum housing some fifty thousand people, the ghosts scrambled up ladders, ran along walkways, through alleys and streets that never saw natural light, wondering if they were indeed still in hell and had not been allowed their annual holiday at all.

The Festival of the Hungry Ghosts was in full swing.

When the two adults were in bed, the children crept back to the kitchen and hid between the refrigerator and the wall where a dark shadow always dwelt, even when the lamp was on. They had the feeling that something was going to happen during the night and they wanted to be there to witness it.

Sure enough, half an hour later a figure in a white flowing gown entered the kitchen. In the near darkness it paused by the work surface and, after a few moments, began eating sweetmeats from one of the two dishes. The children could hear chewing and the smacking of lips and they nudged one another in the darkness of their hiding place. Only when all the sweetmeats had been devoured, did the white figure leave, floating through the kitchen doorway and down the hall.

An hour after this event a second shape crept through the doorway of the kitchen, felt along the top of the work surface and found the plate of cakes. These were eaten even faster than the sweetmeats. Susie and Tim had to suppress giggles during this feast and pinched each other to stop from laughing out loud.

Eventually, all was still in the household.

The following morning Richard Tang was sitting at the breakfast table when Sara brought in the tea. He looked up from reading his newspaper and took the tray from his wife so that she could sit down opposite. For a while they said nothing to each other and merely busied themselves with pouring and stirring, and any small task the table had to offer.

Finally Richard looked at his wife with a tight wan smile on his face.

'I see Susie ate the cakes you left for her,' he said. 'She must have enjoyed them, especially from that plate. It used to be her favourite, you remember.'

Sara nodded and her lips formed a smile similar to the one on her husband's face.

'And Tim obviously enjoyed your sweetmeats.

The boat on the dish must have reminded him of the times you two went fishing together.'

Externally, the porcelain smiles remained intact, but inside each adult fine cracks spread over their souls like the hairline fissures on a glazed Tsung urn. Their spirits threatened to craze and shatter within, but as if each knew of the other's feelings, they reached across the table, touched fingertips, and saved one another.

When Richard could trust himself to speak again, he said, 'It *was* you that ate the sweetmeats, wasn't it?'

Sara nodded. 'And you, the cakes. That was very thoughtful of you. What a pity we can't keep up the pretence. The children are gone and nothing can bring them back – but still, it was kind of you, my husband.'

'My wife.'

They touched again, lightly, aware of the two empty chairs on either side of the table, one beside mother, one beside father. They could have talked about the children and the happy times before that terrible fire in their other flat, six months previously. They could have said things like, 'When the children were alive . . . ' But neither parent was ready for such a large step. After all, the children had only been dead six months, and wounds like that take years, even decades, to close.

At least the Festival of the Hungry Ghosts was over and there would be no more roadside fires to rekindle terrible memories for another year.

Outside, a humid August heat brought hell to the streets.

Changelings

There was a time when fairies were in evidence all over the land. Not just pretty little creatures with gossamer wings (though there were *some* of those) but pixies, gnomes, elves, goblins and other creatures of moor and forest. I think that's why no one believes in them these days, because they are rarely, if ever around. This is not because these creatures no longer exist. It's the woodlands and moors that have gone. How many unspoiled forests are there in *your* county? How many people do you know that live out on the moors? Even villages have been swallowed up by towns. These days most of us dwell in cities and suburbs, where it is highly unlikely that you'll find any little people, and before you scoff ask yourself how many pine martens you've seen since you were born. *They* still exist, hiding in their hollow trees or rock fissures: small grey-brown creatures like weasels, with cream-coloured bibs that change to orange with the leaves in autumn. Have you stopped believing in pine martens too?

Anyway, this story is not about now, but about an earlier time when those forests did exist and the people who inhabited them. In those days there were in the county of Buckinghamshire, men called 'bodgers' who lived in the beech forests. It was the job of the bodgers to care for the trees and to season and roughly hew the timber before it went to be made into furniture. Such famous chairs as the wheelbacks were made from the beechwood cut by bodgers. Bodgers were also responsible for coppicing and pollarding the trees, which means cutting them down to stumps, or shortened trunks, so that they may sprout fresh green crowns. The fairies of the forest did not like their trees being cut, in any way whatsoever, for good or bad.

In the village of Holmer Green, above the town of High Wycombe, two sisters were raised on a farm. The elder one hated farm life, getting up at dawn, milking the cows and collecting the eggs, and she married a rich toy manufacturer and went to live in the town, where she found herself to be remarkably happy.

The younger sister, whose name was Sarah, loved country life. She enjoyed rising early and seeing the sky change from mottled reds and purples to grey or blue. There were so many birds about at that time of day, all marking their territories with jealous songs, that Sarah grew up singing with them. Sarah fell in love with Stephen Kingly, a local bodger, and they were married one May. They went to live in the forest, in Stephen's log cabin, close to the huts where the bodgers carried out their work. She came to love the smell of sawdust and woodshavings, the fresh growth, and the creatures of the woodlands. While her sister was given diamonds, Sarah had nothing but the morning dewdrops. While Sarah walked barefoot on carpets of leaves and grasses, her sister tripped around on Indian rugs. While her sister had orchids delivered to her doorstep, Sarah had but cuckoo-pints and bluebells.

Yet both sisters were happy with their different lives.

Sarah's sister did not want children. She considered them messy little barbarians who hampered one's social life and in any case there were far too many of the boisterous creatures in the world.

The one thing Sarah wanted to make her happiness complete, was a child of her own. Her husband, who was as roughly hewn as the beechwood he fashioned, was a kindly man with a face given to crinkling at the least amusing thing. He told Sarah he wanted to be a father and that they should waste no time in starting a family.

'However,' he said, 'I think it's better you don't have the baby here, in the forest, but go to the town where care is to be had should things not go to plan. You're a fine healthy lass with bloom on your cheeks, but I'd feel righter and better if you was in good hands. I can coppice a tree with the best of 'em, but babies is outside my experience, if you see what I mean. Your sister's is the best place for you.'

Sarah was not so sure her sister would approve of all that the birth of a baby required, but when she was eight months pregnant she took herself down to High Wycombe, where her elder sister greeted her and was actually delighted to be of assistance. As long as it wasn't her giving birth, she wasn't in the least concerned. In fact she said she was quite looking forward to being an aunt.

'Aunts get the best of the little brutes,' she said. 'They can send them home when they get too much.'

Sarah returned to Stephen with their son, a child

with her blue eyes and his broad brow. The baby was placed in a cradle of beechwood, freshly carpentered, with acorns carved in the headboard and side-spokes that had been turned on a bodger's lathe fashioned from a springy branch, a piece of string and a twig for a foot pedal.

The night after Sarah's return from High Wycombe, the fairies came out of their hiding places in the forest, and crept up to the window of the cabin. With jealous hearts they stared through the window at the human child, lying in its new cradle. Fairies come into this world fully grown and if there's one thing they envy humans for, it's the ability to produce babies. They itched to get their fingers on the cherub, with its rosy cheeks and plump arms. They were consumed with a desire to hold it in their arms and pass it to one another and rock it to sleep. They were desperate to possess this human baby.

'We must have it,' they groaned, pressing their faces against the glass window, their chlorophyll breath greening the morning air. 'The frosts are coming. We must have this baby to keep us warm in our nests. We *need* this human child more than its parents. This is our forest, not theirs, and everything in it belongs to us. They have *our* baby . . .' And so it went on, fairy logic being wholly concerned with providing the fairies with excuses to take what they wanted and never a mention of 'theft' or 'robbery' or 'stealing' came into their arguments.

Among their number the fairies had a Robin Goodfellow, a Pook from the county of Cornwall, who is the only one of the little creatures able to travel vast distances. He had the facility of being able to transform himself into an animal, and this he did, imitating the form of Stephen Kingly's household dog. In this guise he entered the cabin and snatched the baby from its bed, making off with it into the forest. When the child was safely in the hands of the fairyfolk, the Pook carried a sickly elf back to the cabin, and put him in the cradle, still warm from the baby.

This exchange is common practice amongst the fairies.

When Sarah first saw the sickly elf, with its sunken cheeks and feverish eyes, its hunched back and rickety legs, she did not guess what had happened. The fairies have a trick of leaving an aura round the changeling, so that the humans see their own baby. So though the changeling had stick-thin arms, Sarah saw only plump chubby limbs. Where the changeling had sallow skin, Sarah saw a pink, unblemished complexion. Though the creature in her arms had a knobbled head and large ugly feet, Sarah saw only the brow of her husband, her own dainty feet. She loved and cared for the changeling as she would have done her own child and it was only when the elf died, one night when the snow was piled against the cabin door, that she realized what had happened. In death the aura left by the fairies fell away from the changeling and its true form was revealed to the despairing mother.

Meanwhile, in the forest, the pixies and goblins and other races of fairyfolk were up to their usual tricks.

They took any tools left lying around by the bodgers and hid them under the snow. They lowered the well bucket at night, so that it froze fast in the ice. They frightened the chickens, pretending to be foxes, so that the hens would not lay. They knocked over unattended milk churns and greened the cheeses with their breath.

And they had the baby.

Now a human baby in fairy hands remains a baby. They do not allow it to grow into an infant, adolescent and finally adult human, because they have no use for such creatures. So Sarah's child grew not a day older over that winter, and was passed around the fairies like the parcel in the party game. They thrilled to the simple idea of possessing something which belonged to the humans, something they had taken, and there was not even a thought for the poor elf who had been sacrificed. When the changeling died the fairies shrugged their shoulders and said, 'Well, it would have died *anyway*, whether it was here or there. It was sick, wasn't it?'

They danced, they performed mischief, they annoyed the owls and irritated the squirrels, and did all the things that fairies do and have done since their first witenagemot in the year of nought. They took wych-hazel seeds and put them down the bodgers' shirts when they were resting and threw couch-grass darts into the washing that hung on Sarah's line. They took bedstraw weeds and planted them amongst Sarah's vegetables, so that the latter were choked. They sent beetles into the cabin to click away behind the wainscot and keep the humans awake at night.

Changelings

They simply behaved like fairies.

At the end of the winter Sarah suddenly announced to Stephen that she was going to have another child.

'We want this baby to be healthy,' she said, 'so I'm going to go to my sister's early. I hate to leave you all alone for the spring, Stephen, but this is best, don't you agree?'

'Don't you worry about me,' said her husband. 'I can take care of myself all right. I've lived in the forest since I was fourteen and looked after myself until we got married, so I can do well without a woman around, though I'll miss you of course.'

He touched her cheek with a hand rough from planing and rubbing wood with sandpaper.

'I'll miss you of course.'

So Sarah went to her sister's house in the town again and stayed there the whole summer. When the autumn came around, she returned to the forest. The leaves were boating on the currents of air and flashing their red and gold in the thin shafts of sunlight that penetrated the canopies of beech. Proudly she presented her husband with the new baby, a child of truly wondrous beauty. It had chubby apple-red cheeks and a milky complexion. Its eyes were a vivid blue and bright as stars. It chuckled and chortled and kicked its legs whenever it was tickled and blew bubbles of spit with its cupid's bow mouth.

The fairies were insane with envy and called for a witenagemot under the largest beech in the forest.

'You see what they've done?' screeched a hobgoblin.

'They've palmed us off with this second-rate baby, not nearly as handsome as the child they have now, and we can't do a thing about it. They know we can only give them *one* changeling and now we're stuck with this baby which isn't a patch on theirs.'

They gathered under the beech trees, amongst the rotting fungi, and fumed and raged, kicking petulantly at innocent toads, and stamping on the tails of damsel flies. When the fairies have tantrums the whole forest knows about it.

Suddenly a knowledgeable wight, well versed in fairy law, came up with an answer.

'Stop this cavorting for a minute and listen to me! There is one thing we can do. We can exchange the baby we've got, for the second child. It's the only and final exchange permitted to us, so we have to be sure we want it. Do we want this new baby?'

There was a general roar of assent which frightened the rooks and sent them up to blacken the sky.

That night the Pook became an owl and flew down the chimney of the cabin while the couple were fast asleep. It put the baby it had in its beak into the cradle and snatched up the second child. Then it flew back up the chimney and into the night, where the fairies were waiting impatiently for their new glossy-skinned little plum of a child. They received it into their many tiny arms.

They placed it on a pile of autumn leaves and under the harvest moon, studied their new possession. One of the fairies reached out and patted the baby's head, as loving aunts and uncles are wont to do.

Suddenly, a transformation began to take place.

There was a whirring, clicking sound coming from within the child. Its arms began to move outwards *tik-tik-tik* and its head downwards *tok-tok-tok*. Mechanical movements that startled the fairies and made them step back to watch the transformation in utter horror.

The cheeks of the baby sucked inwards and became hollow. Its skin turned a yellowish hue. Its eyes shrunk and became wizened around the edges, while its limbs stretched and narrowed to become knobbly sticks, all twisted and bent. Its back arched slowly until there was a noticeable hunch, while its shoulders dropped and its chest caved. Finally its breathing shallowed to a mere whisper that would hardly stir a dead leaf.

The fairies stood around this creature, stunned by the knowledge that a simple farm girl had tricked them. They, who had all the deviousness that nature could devise in any creature, natural or otherwise, had been duped by a human who had not even the sense to marry a rich toymaker as her sister had done. A woman who had married an illiterate bodger whose only talents were in whittling beechwood and carving clothes pegs as a present for his wife. A woman who had nothing but a log cabin and a cheerful disposition.

This woman had fooled the whole fairy nation, and there was nothing they could do about it.

Under the bright contemptuous glare of the moon, the plump child they had stolen from its cradle now looked for all the world like a sickly elf.

The Orkney Trows

On a cold first-of-December night when the seas were clawing the rocky coastline of Hoy, one of the Orkney Islands, a fisherman left his wife and son in their croft and set out with his nets to find herring. The fisherman's name was Ben Kirk and he had lived in the Orkneys all his life. Indeed he had been born in the turf and stone croft which now kept his own family from the ravages of the northern climate. He owned very little in the way of possessions, but he had his skiff with its small sail, his precious nets and a pocket-knife given to him by his uncle. His wife Morag had brought with her into the marriage a wonderful grandfather clock. This marvellous device was made of rosewood and had a German movement that kept time to the minute. Its hands were crinkled on purpose, like tiny wavy swords, and the pendulum was of solid bronze. Every quarter of an hour the great clock spoke to the room in accents of sounding brass and tinkling cymbal.

Ben loved the smell of peat burning in the stone fireplace, and the sound of the wind in the crags, and a calm sea on a rare tranquil day. As for Orkney, he neither loved nor hated it, for he never thought about it one way or the other. Orkney was part of him and you don't consider whether you love your own arm or your leg, you take these things for granted.

Once he had pushed his skiff out into the turbulent waters, he knew that it was going to be a rough night. The ocean off the north Scottish coastline is seldom still, but Ben was descended from Scandinavian ancestors, the kind of people who had set sail in longships to found colonies on Iceland and Greenland. He had savage seas in his blood. With his lamp on the prow of the boat to guide him, he rowed his craft out into the Pentland Firth, where the shoals were said to be that night, and then raised the sail.

Just as the dawn came to grey the waters of the firth, a squall swept suddenly down from the Shetlands. Ben had the sail up and tried to lower it quickly, before the erratic winds caught it broadside. While he was standing, trying to loosen a wet knot on a sheet, the craft capsized and threw him into the foaming seas. He was unable to swim to his upturned skiff, and his heavy oilskins and seaman's boots dragged him down. His sou'wester floated away on the waves.

When Ben's twelve-year-old son, Alisdair, found the skiff washed up on the Hoy shore the following morning, he knew his father had been drowned. The nets were still attached to the boat, though they had been badly damaged. Further down the coastline, he found his father's yellow sou'wester, and this item of seaman's clothing confirmed his fears. He went home to tell his poor mother, who took it badly, though all fishermen's wives hang on the edge of the night expecting such news to come with the dawn.

When the grief was over, Alisdair told his mother

that he was going to repair his father's boat and begin fishing. Alisdair suggested to his mother that they might sell the grandfather clock, to buy more nets, but this upset her so much he refrained from mentioning it again. Instead, he asked her to help him mend the old nets and hoped they would stay together for a few more years. They also had to make a new sail, for the old one had been lost. Although she feared for her son, his mother knew that someone had to do the fishing or they would both starve. Indeed, Ben had taken Alisdair with him many times, and had himself begun the fisherman's life at the age of thirteen or so.

Thus young Alisdair became what his father had been and his grandfather before him, and though he missed Ben sorely, he did not complain nor question his lot. He stoically followed tradition and thought only of the cod and herring.

'We must keep oursen from hunger, Mither,' he said, 'for I widna wish us tae end up begging on the streets of Edinburgh.'

When the summer came around, the hard life of the fisherman became a little easier. Sometimes, Alisdair even looked forward to chasing the waves and took pride in the fact that he had mastered the skiff until he could manage the sheets and tiller almost as well as his father had done. His catches were moderate, but adequate.

One evening, when the sun was purpling the waters of the firth, Alisdair began casting and drawing his nets. As he was hauling in a reasonable catch and silver danced on the surface of the sea, he heard a harsh-sounding voice.

'Fetch me the magic!'

Looking up the boy was startled to see a small stumpy dwarf standing on a rock. The little creature had long green hair hanging like sea-bed fronds to his ankles and his eyes were like two small cockleshells. In appearance neither old nor young, the dwarf seemed outside of age. He pointed a knobbly finger at the shore and repeated his demand as the waves swilled over his precarious platform. He splashed himself as he stamped his foot.

'Fetch me the magic! Now!'

It was at that moment that Alisdair realized who, or rather what the creature was. It was a trow, a sea-trow in fact, a supernatural being distantly related to the trolls of Norway. How often had he heard the fishwives shrieking at naughty children, 'Trow tak' ye!' as the infants harried their mothers to distraction.

Now here was one in the flesh, handing out commands. It would not do to disobey, though Alisdair felt the need to protest.

'But the fishing's gude. It wud be a shame tae leave it sae soon. Widna later be better?'

'No, it wouldn't at all,' shrieked the trow. '*Now* would be better. *Now* is the only time. I want the magic *now*.' And with these words the sea-trow did a frantic dance on the rock, his legs and arms moving furiously. A heavy swell began to grow and assisted the skiff shoreward. The nets which had been on the lee side of the boat, were suddenly to windward and in danger of being overrun. Alisdair hastily hauled them all the way in and allowed the craft to be carried to the beach. Once there he leapt out of the boat and began to search the rocks and sand, not really knowing what he was looking for.

He found a huge shell and thought that this was what the trow wanted. Running to the boat he jumped in and rowed to where the sea-trow was standing. He handed him the large whelk.

'What's this?' cried the trow, throwing the shell at least a mile out to sea. 'I want the magic. Get me the magic!'

'Whut does the magic look like?' shouted Alisdair, but his words were lost in the noisy wind that blew his skiff immediately back to the shore.

He searched the area again and discovered a shiny stone quite unlike any others on the beach. It had red veins running through it like frozen forked lightning. He had never seen a pebble like it before in all his Orkney days.

'This *must* be the magic,' he said to himself.

Once again he dashed to his boat, and once he was in it the waves carried him out to where the trow was standing with arms folded over his chest, muttering and grumbling into his seaweed hair.

On being handed the pebble, the trow's nostrils dilated to cavernous proportions and Alisdair thought the little man's head was going to explode, for it expanded to twice its original size. The pebble went the way of the shell, only this time Alisdair was sure it would end up on the shores of mainland Scotland.

The whisper from the trow was terrifying.

'You wish to be a sea slug?'

'No, sir,' said Alisdair, trembling.

'A ragworm perhaps?'

'Not that either, sir.'

'THEN GET ME THE MAGIC, YOU IMBECILE!' came the screech that had the boat-following herring gulls wheeling away in panic.

'Please, sir,' quaked Alisdair, 'whut does the magic look like?'

The trow's voice became quite reasonable, though he looked up at the rapidly darkening sky with some concern written on his brow.

'It's in a bottle, half-buried in the sand.'

'Thank you, sir,' said Alisdair, relieved. 'I'll fetch it straight.'

This time the boy had to row back to the beach and once on the shore he searched the rocks and pools in the gloaming until a dull gleam caught his eye. There was the container, buried to its neck, by one of the rock pools. He dug it out. It was of mottled green glass, with a fishnet cover and a crumbling cork. Shaped like a cod bottle, with a rounded base, its neck and sides were ribbed. Alisdair had seen such bottles washed up on the shore before, not realizing they had once contained magic.

He hurried back to the boat and began rowing out to the rock. Inside the bottle the liquid swashed back and forth. It was, he guessed, about a quarter full.

The sea was quite still now and the wind had dropped to a gentle breeze. By the time he got to his destination, the darkness had deepened to a heavy purple and he was surprised to see the surface of the rock bare. He looked around, thinking he had got the wrong one, but no, there was no other rock to be seen. The trow had gone, leaving Alisdair with the magic.

He thought about throwing it overboard, into the sea, thinking perhaps that was what the trow might wish him to do, but changed his mind.

'I'll keep it in the boat, so ah will,' he said to himself, 'and if the wee chap comes back, he can have it.'

On reaching the croft, Alisdair said nothing to his mother. He simply ate his dinner of tatties and neaps, had a cup of tea, and sat looking at the clock with its dignified Roman numerals and the curlicued hands moving slowly towards another whirring, clicking prelude to a short speech from the chimes.

Over the next few months Alisdair was sorely tempted to open the bottle and to try to use some of the magic inside. The nets were falling apart and the fish were escaping through the holes. The boat leaked, where it had been repaired by him, because he and his mother had been unable to afford proper caulking material. All he needed to do was uncork the bottle and use just a drop of the strange green liquid. In fact, he did take out the stopper, just once, to sniff the opening. It smelled of heather and herbs and spices, so strongly it made his nose wrinkle.

However, he resisted the urge to help himself. The magic was not his to use. It belonged to the trows and should they ever ask for it back, he wanted to return it to them untouched. Indeed, he saw himself as a kind of guardian of fairy magic. He was storing it for the little creatures, ready for the time when they would appear before him and demand it back. He was a trustworthy boy, one who had been raised with good manners and fine morals.

Later in the season, the shoals increased in number and despite the bad condition of the nets, Alisdair was able to take home several good catches, which his mother carried to the market and sold. When winter came again, the trow still had not appeared, so Alisdair took the bottle home and kept it on the mantelpiece, where it was safe from being lost overboard in a storm.

On the thirtieth of November, the evening before the anniversary of his father's drowning, Alisdair was sitting by a high peat fire warming himself before going out to his vessel. His mother was already in bed and fast asleep. The clock was ticking quietly, making the only regular noise in the room. In the grate the peat hissed blue and green flames, as if it were hiding tiny dragons in its dark folds.

Suddenly, the door rattled. It was not a knock, as one would expect from a neighbour or friend, but Alisdair had the distinct impression that the movement was not caused by the wind, that someone was outside and wanting to get in. When it happened again, he went to the small mean window and peered through the bullseye panes. The misshapen glass warped the figure under the stoop, standing on the slab of granite his mother called her 'steps', but Alisdair recognised it straight away.

It was the trow.

He lifted the sneck and opened the thick wooden door. The trow pushed past him and stared about the room.

'Where is it?' snapped the little creature. His long unkempt hair was now a bracken brown, though it still hung to his ankles and his bumpy nose poked through the curtains it formed over his ugly face. 'Where's the magic my brother made you fetch?'

'Your brother?' said Alisdair.

'Of course, my brother, of course,' rattled the trow. 'Don't you recognise a land-trow from a sea-trow, you idiot? Brown and green. Brown and green. I'm land, he's sea. Ah.' He pointed to the mantelpiece. 'There it is.'

'Aye, there it is,' remarked Alisdair, 'safe and sound.'

'Have you used any?' asked the trow, jumping a metre off the flagstones and snatching the bottle. The enquiry was so matter-of-fact Alisdair realized at once that nothing would have happened to him if he had taken some of the magic. The trows had obviously expected him to use some for himself.

'Nary a drap,' he replied, 'but I wid like . . .'

'Good, good,' snapped the trow, wrenching the stopper from the bottle and sniffing. Then the expression on his pocked face changed and he looked up at Alisdair with slit-shell eyes.

'It's gone,' he said, 'all of it.'

'*Whut*?' cried the boy in distress. 'It cannae have. Ah hav'nae touched it and ahm certain sure my mother hasnae either. We wudnae meddle with fairy magic, honest.'

'Visitors?' questioned the trow, clearly believing him.

'None that have been left alane.'

'Ahhh,' said the trow.

Alisdair cried, 'Whut then?'

The trow shook his head.

'It's evaporated,' he stated. 'The cork's crumbling. Peat burning fiercely down below. Warm room. It's gone and evaporated.'

'Ahm sorry,' said Alisdair.

'No matter,' cried the little creature briskly. 'I'll just have to collect it up again. Open the door, put out the fire, let the cold air in.' He pointed to some droplets of moisture on the bullseye panes. 'The magic has condensed on the cold window glass. We'll turn it to ice and then I'll scrape it off and put it back in the bottle. No harm done.'

Alisdair did as he was told, dousing the fire and then opening the door to let the winter air into the room. Soon it was freezing inside and a frost-fern pattern formed on the window panes. The trow busied himself, scraping away with a little knife and putting his scrapings into the neck of the bottle. Finally he stopped.

'That's that then. Any left over you can keep.'

With that the creature ran through the doorway and up into the crags of the hillside, without a word of gratitude or thanks.

Alisdair closed the door, relit the fire, and then went to the window. As he had guessed there was not a crystal of ice or frost left on the panes. The land-trow had taken all there was.

The boy sighed and settled back in his chair, staring into the flames coming from the peat. After some time had gone by, the grandfather clock chimed, and Alisdair looked up into its face.

He started, suddenly.

There on the glass were several droplets of moisture.

Just as he was rising, hoping to put out the fire before they disappeared, the droplets ran down the glass and into the German works of the ancient timepiece. Alisdair reached for the face-panel, but the magic had definitely gone. He fell back in his chair in despair.

Yet, as he stared at the clock, something strange began to take place. The wiggly hands started to move backwards. At first they were slow and smooth, but then they began to whizz round at a terrific rate, until they were spinning so fast Alisdair could not see them. The chimes began to zither out, until they formed one continuous note. It hurt his ears and he would have put his hands over them but they seemed pinned to his side. He felt sick and dizzy and longed to lie down but somehow he was frozen to the chair. The giddiness overwhelmed him, until he could no longer keep his eyes open and had to sit out the happening with them tightly shut.

It seemed to go on for a very long time.

When he opened his eyes again, the room was very still. He looked up at the clock face, to see that the hands stood at a quarter to ten. It was dark outside. The hurricane lamp burned above the rickety table. Just as the quarter chimes filled the silence, the door opened . . . and in stepped his father, brushing snowflakes from his oilskins.

'Still up, laddie?'

'Aye, Fether,' said Alisdair, almost in a whisper.

'Well, it's time you were a-bed. Ahm off for the fishing, mind, so away ye go.'

Alisdair rose as if in a dream and made towards his small alcove at the back of the room, a kind of shelf cut into the stone of the croft. When he reached it a thought struck him and he turned and said, 'Whut date is it today, Fether?'

'Date?' His father scratched his head. 'Ahm no sure.' Then his eyes brightened. 'Aye, it's the first. The first of December, to be sure. Why d'ye ask, laddie? Is it the end of school that prompts these questions?' and Ben laughed at his son, his face crinkling like sea-sand rippled by the wavelets.

'Somethin' like that,' answered Alisdair, but though he dare not ask for further information, he knew for certain sure what had happened and why his father was still alive. The magic in the clock had turned time back a whole year. It was the eve of his father's death. The tragedy was still to take place, the following morning. Ben was about to venture out, to be drowned in the storm.

'Stay home tonight, Fether,' cried Alisdair. 'I'm feared for ye. There's a gie big storm brewin'.'

His father looked shocked at this outburst.

'Laddie, laddie, get a hold o' yersen,' said his father softly. 'Ye ken ah cannae stay home. There's the fishing to be done.'

And with that, Ben turned and went through the croft doorway, on his way down to the sea strand.

Alisdair leapt from his bed and followed his father out into the night. His feet flew over the turf as he raced to the beach where the boat was moored. Reaching the spot well before his father, he gathered up the nets and raced into the hills. Ben, open-mouthed, watched as his son climbed up into the darkness and out of sight. When he found his skiff empty of nets, Ben was terribly angry, and went home to his croft threatening all sorts of retribution on his son. However, before Alisdair had returned the next morning, the fisherman had risen from his bed and met other Orkney men on the beaches. In the shark-coloured dawn he had manned a lifeboat, launched to save fellow seamen from the gale that was raging out on the waters. Several boats had been lost at sea and it was a miracle, said one fisherman, that no one had gone down with them. Ben guessed that his son had received some kind of premonition, a warning that the squall was about to hit the firth, and he returned home in a very different frame of mind.

When Alisdair came back with the nets and offered him an apology, Ben said sternly, 'Ah ken fine ye were concerned for ma welfare, son, but in future ah must be ma own judge.'

'Aye, Fether,' replied the lad, and they shook hands gravely, man and boy, each knowing what he knew and never telling the other, though they fished together side by side for more than forty-seven years from that day.

Scarecrows

There is a coastal village out on the salt marshes of Essex, one of those places with a name ending in *ness*, which apart from something to do with 'nose' means it is remote enough to distrust strangers.

This village is called Feerness. It sits on an alluvial island which can be reached at low tide from the mainland by a track known locally as 'the hard'. The hard is visible for just a short period each day, the rest of the time it is submerged. A horseman crossing the hard needs to judge when to start his journey very accurately, while the waters are still on the ebb, to reach the other side before the tide turns and rushes back in to recover its territory.

Many are those who wished to visit Feerness and have misjudged the speed of the incoming tidal rays, and have drowned with the *rhonking* of geese in their ears. The sea geese that feed on the mudflats have never yet been known to set to and save a victim of the cruel eddies and currents that clutch even the strongest of swimmers, dragging them down to a long cold sleep.

The saltings around the island are fond of mists and marsh fogs. There are strange creeks there, where the yellowish scummy water has not been changed since the dark ages, and where boats have stuck and men have been sucked to horrible deaths. In such places of course, there are still nooks of magic, which have not been cleared away by the march of reason and logic of later centuries. They lie there in hollows, like pockets of green marsh gas, waiting to be used up.

Thus, the villagers of Feerness had never needed to discourage strangers from visiting their island. The sea and surrounding bogs had done that for them. However, with the invention of four-wheel-drive vehicles, they found they were being invaded every spring and summer. The speed of these vehicles, compared with horse-drawn carriages, enabled outsiders to cross the hard quickly and safely, and in large numbers.

Those visitors that forced their way into the otherwise closed community, which had been inbred for well over ten centuries, were heard to remark what a pretty village it was.

'Aren't the houses charming?' remarked the foreigners. 'Look at the beautiful gabled windows and the thatched rooftops of the cottages. Have you seen the gardens? Full of hollyhocks and roses, and trellises covered in wisteria. And the bullseye windows and leaded lights . . .'

The island itself was flat and bleak, with muddy inlets that smelled of saltwort and bladder-wrack. There were rotting hulks stuck in the sludge, exposed at low tide, where oyster catchers and dunlin congregated. The overpowering odour was of decaying shellfish, since the farmers used crushed cockleshells to spread on their fields. Always, a cold wind straight from Siberia cut through the reeds like a scythe, winter and summer.

It was only the dwellings themselves that were

attractive to outsiders, not the location or the landscape.

So the villagers had a meeting one night, and being fisher and farming folk, decided on a course of action congruent with their way of life. They were simple people who believed in simple solutions. They rebuilt their village, making it ugly and frightening, using stone dredged from the slick wastes of the estuary, and sea-rotted timbers covered in limpets and barnacles. There were bulges, and mean little windows as tight as ploughshare slits in turnips, and sills dripping with slime. There were grotesques jutting from the eaves, and dark bands of pocked wood, and misshapen bricks of river mud sealed with organic sludge. The gardens grew only stunted alders, always leafless, that twisted in arthritic poses. There were stagnant pools and lifeless streams, and mounds reminiscent of unkempt graves.

These new houses threw daunting shadows that in themselves were forbidding areas, cold as churchyard earth.

The visiting vehicles stopped coming.

One night, a villager by the name of John Barnes was sitting in an armchair by his cottage fire, listening to the delicate chimes of his grandfather's pocketwatch. A paraffin lamp burned by his side. Outside the rain was striking the window-slats as if it were lead shot. A wind gusted around the chimney stack, ever complaining of its tribulations. It was inclement weather and John Barnes was glad to be out of it.

Suddenly there was a knocking on the door, wood on wood, someone using a stick.

Grumbling, he rose from his armchair and went to see who would brave such a storm in order to see a neighbour. When he lifted the sneck, the door flew open to reveal the scarecrow he had put out in the fields only three days before. The figure was wearing a discarded hat which once belonged to John's aunt, the brim of which formed channels for rivulets of rainwater. Damp straw was plastered to the turnip brow and dripped on to an already sodden coat that had seen at least a century. In his hand was a stout hickory.

Empty eyesockets stared. The sawtoothed mouth looked grim.

'What on earth do you want?' asked the astonished John Barnes. It was not the idea that his scarecrow stood before him which was shocking, so much as the fact that the fellow had deserted his post and left the fields unattended.

'This house,' said the scarecrow, 'was obviously built for the likes of me, not people like you. You must have stolen it from my ancestors. I'm reclaiming my rights.'

With that, strong gloved fingers of straw gripped John Barnes by the shoulder and wrenched him out into the rain. The scarecrow stepped inside the cottage and slammed the door. There were the sounds of bolts being slammed into place and after a few moments the lamp was put out and the fire doused.

John Barnes stood there for quite some time, hardly able to believe what had happened. When he finally recovered his wits, he was soaked through. He could still hear the rain rattling on the slats, but the house was in darkness.

Thrown out of his own home by his scarecrow!

John became incensed and started banging on the door, then on the small windows. He began yelling loudly, threatening the scarecrow, and telling it to come outside and fight.

Suddenly, the door to the cottage flew open again, and the scarecrow reappeared with his hickory stick to give John Barnes such a ferocious look that the man ran off, over the fields, to the house of his neighbour Albert Renkin.

Albert met him halfway between the two houses. He too was in his shirtsleeves and soaked to the skin. On his face was a look of tragic indignation. John guessed what had happened, even before Albert opened his mouth.

'The wife's gone down to the vicar,' said Albert, 'to get help. We can't have this! Scarecrows turning us out of our own homes. I allus treated mine fair. They had a full season out in the fields, never less, and a new face when the rooks had picked holes in the old one. Why, I even gave one a scarf that were only twenty year old, once. There's gratitud' for yer!'

John was equally condemning of *his* scarecrow, whom he had created with his own hands just a few days previously.

'You give them an existence, and they want a life!' complained John. 'It's allus the same in this world. Folks are never satisfied with their station. They allus wants more . . .'

The two men stopped talking, for in the distance they heard the wail of other villagers, all lamenting the gross unfairness of being evicted from their homes by scarecrows. It was a bad night and worse to come.

Three days later, the villagers were still no nearer to recovering their homes. Even the local trading store had a usurper behind the counter, and this *thing*, with its black hollow eyes and jaggedy mouth, refused to serve any human being.

'Bloomin' cheek of it,' cried the storekeeper, Alex Wiles. 'Can't even buy somethin' at me own store.'

The only building which had not been taken over was the church, because this was the one edifice they had not altered into a grotesque. Here the humans huddled together for warmth at night, and talked in whispers of regaining their homes.

'We've been occupied, by an army of scarecrows that don't know their place,' snarled John Barnes, 'and I for one an't going to stand for it.'

One of the more liberal ladies present spoke up.

'Perhaps we should offer them something better for the future? Promise them a longer life? What do you think? It can't be much fun for them, standing out in a field, waving at birds. It's cold and damp, even on the best of nights, and the morning mists must be awful for their chests . . .'

'We'll promise 'em somethin' all right,' muttered Alex Wiles, darkly. 'In the meantime, I have to admit it were our own faults. We made the houses look attractive to 'em, sort of encouraged 'em to hop down off their poles and march down to chuck us out. If the houses wasn't scary, they wouldn't want 'em, I'm sure. We can't get inside, but we can work on the outsides.'

He explained his plan to the rest of the villagers.

John Barnes was commissioned to go across to the mainland. He waited until the tide was right, then set off with a pony and trap, over the hard. The sea came back in again, and then retreated once more, and John Barnes returned with his purchase. The villagers had clubbed together and had bought over five hundred litres of whitewash, with which they intended to paint the cottages. Brushes were found in barns, and ladders in sheds. Man, woman and child got to work, licking the stonework of the cottages with the paintbrushes. Once in a while a scarecrow would come to the window, to stare out at the activity, but Albert Renkin had ensured that every group of painters had an open fire going, with flaming brands ready to hand. Scarecrows are terrified of fire, and none of them dared venture outside to chase away the decorators.

Finally, all the cottages were a blinding white, the aspect of their exteriors quite transformed. Where they had looked makeshift and unsightly, they now looked quite pretty. It was true that they still seemed a little misshapen, but the strange lumpiness was almost invisible to the eye now, and the narrow windows had borders round them making them blend more with the stonework. The gargoyles had been removed from the gutters and any projections levelled. After they had finished, it was clear to the villagers that the scarecrows were feeling uncomfortable in their new white soft-looking dwellings. They kept coming to the windows and looking out, their expressions no longer savage, but wistful.

Three days later a message came from the scarecrows, asking the villagers to pick a meeting place, to sort out their differences.

'We just want a fair deal,' said the scarecrows. 'We know this has upset you, but we want to work out better arrangements for ourselves in the future. We're fed up with being stuck on a crossframe out in the fields, left out in all weathers to bake or flap in the wind and the rain, hanging there by our arms, crucified for all to see . . . ' It went on in the same vein.

John Barnes accepted the terms on behalf of the villagers and said that the best place to meet the scarecrows would be on neutral ground. If they met in the cottages, there would be advantages to one side, and if they met in the fields, advantages to the other.

'We shall meet on the hard,' said John Barnes, 'between the village and the mainland.'

To the scarecrows this sounded like a sensible solution to the problem of where to talk, but then scarecrows are not familiar with the deviousness of men.

The scarecrows arrived on the hard, midway between the village and the mainland, at the appointed time. However, the villagers themselves were not there, and never did come. What came in their place was a spring tide, which swept away the scarecrows, carrying them off over the sea to France, where they were tossed on to Normandy beaches by the waves. There they ended their days, broken and scattered, amongst match boxes, seaweed,

110

driftwood, bottles and other flotsam and jetsam.

The villagers were of course triumphant and stormed back into their newly whitewashed houses, glad to be human beings with brains, and not hollow turnip heads. John Barnes settled once more to his old way of life, without remorse, as did his neighbour Albert Renkin, and indeed all the villagers of Feerness.

The summer went by without a scarecrow being erected in the fields. The crows and rooks and seagulls had a glorious time, but the villagers were not going to be caught twice. They would rather lose a bit of seed, a few crops, than their cottages.

'Why, next time we might not get 'em back,' said Alex Wiles. '*Things* probably learn tricks, as quickly as people, once they've been had by 'em!'

Winter came in and frost was on the land. Just before Christmas, John Barnes hitched up his pony and trap, and crossed the hard to the mainland to fetch some special stores. He wanted oranges and nuts for his Christmas feast, and one or two other bits and bobs. He had to wait until three o'clock in the morning for the tide to change, so that he could get back across the hard. As he waited, the snow came down in thick gobbets to cover the land.

It was not long after his chiming pocketwatch struck three that he set forth, his trap wheels leaving twin furrows in the snow behind him. When he was halfway across, he was met by the villagers of Feerness, coming the other way. He was astonished to see that they were in their pyjamas and nightgowns and had no shoes on their feet, for it was bitterly cold out on the wastes.

'What on earth has happened?' he asked Albert Renkin.

'Ah, don't ask, don't ask,' wailed his neighbour, 'but since you do, well, you remember we painted the cottages, so they was all white and soft-looking? This evening, the children of the village was out in their gardens, and o' course, wanting a bit of fun, they built these snowmen . . .'